discover libraries

This book should be returned on or before the due date.

To renew or order library books please telephone 01522 782010
or visit https://lincolnshire.spydus.co.uk

You will require a Personal Identification Number.
Ask any member of staff for this.

The above does not apply to Reader's Group Collection Stock.

1 3 5 7 9 10 8 6 4 2

Young Arrow
20 Vauxhall Bridge Road
London SW1V 2SA

Young Arrow is part of the Penguin Random House group of companies
whose addresses can be found at global.penguinrandomhouse.com

Penguin
Random House
UK

First published by Young Arrow in 2018
This edition published in paperback by Young Arrow in 2018

www.penguin.co.uk

A CIP catalogue record for this book
is available from the British Library

ISBN 9781784754051

Printed and bound in Great Britain by
Clays Ltd, Elcograf S.p.A.

Penguin Random House is committed to a sustainable future for our
business, our readers and our planet. This book is made from Forest
Stewardship Council® certified paper.

THE *NERDIEST,* WIMPIEST, DORKIEST I FUNNY EVER

Chapter 1

THE JOKE HEARD ROUND THE WORLD

So, have you ever been in exactly the wrong place at exactly the wrong time?

For instance, have you ever tried to tell jokes to people who don't speak your language, which means they'll never laugh because they don't understand a single word you're saying?

This is why I'm sweating like a berserk Super Soaker.

This is also why I probably shouldn't've accepted the invitation to address the United Nations. They wanted me to ask the assembled diplomats to play nice with each other for the sake of kids all around the world.

I think the last time some of these guys played nice, there were snakes involved.

Talk about your mission impossible.

Yes, I've done some amazingly incredible stuff in my young life. I've won the first-ever Planet's Funniest Kid stand-up comedian contest even though, technically, I can't stand up. And I wasn't really up against the planet like I am now, just the United States. I have my own TV show on BNC. I've even kissed a few girls.

But telling jokes that'll make all 193 member

states of the UN General Assembly chuckle? It's a nightmare.

"When you think about it," I sputter into my microphone, "we humans are all one big family."

Dozens of translators instantaneously repeat what I just said into the earpieces of hundreds of frowning foreign dignitaries.

I slide into a joke to soften them up. "Speaking of happy families, the other night, I cooked dinner for *my* family. It was going to be a surprise but the fire trucks showing up sort of ruined it."

I smile. Nervously. And wait for the translators to finish my joke for me in all sorts of languages. When they're done, I'm still smiling and sweating but nobody is laughing.

"Why does this boy set his house on fire?" demands one delegate in a thick Slovenian accent.

"Does he ask us to cook dinner for his family?" asks a German lady.

"I object!" proclaims the Chinese ambassador. "The Happy Family is a Chinese dish and must be stir-fried in a wok with bamboo shoots!"

"You guys?" I plead. "It's just a joke!"

"*Sacré bleu!*" screams another diplomat. "Did

3

this boy in the wheelchair call me a joke?" She pounds her desk with a shoe.

"You insult me," cries that Slovenian guy, "and you insult my country."

"Give him the hook!" shouts the American representative to the UN, the lady who invited me to speak in the first place. "Get him offstage!"

Finally, everybody at the United Nations is united around a common cause. They all agree on one thing: I Not Funny.

Chapter 2

TUNNEL OF FEAR

Fortunately, that's when I wake up.

Like I said, me speaking at the United Nations? It's a nightmare. Only I'm having my nightmare in the middle of the day because I grabbed a quick catnap while the crew set up the scenery for the final shot of this season's *Jamie Funnie* TV series. That's one good thing about being stuck in a wheelchair. You always have a comfy seat when you want to nod off.

During the break, Nigel Bigglebottom, the British actor playing the TV version of my uncle Frankie, fixed himself a spot of tea along with some cookies, which he calls biscuits. That still confuses me, along with chips and crisps. Everybody else is guzzling coffee, water, and soda pop. When you work on a TV show, free snacks and beverages are everywhere.

"I can't believe this will be our final scene for the entire season!" Nigel proclaims in a plummy British accent. Everything he says sounds supersnooty, even though he's really friendly. Fortunately, he switches into a New Yawk accent when he plays Uncle Frankie. Otherwise it would just sound weird.

Actually, almost everything about starring in a TV show called *Jamie Funnie* based on my life is kind of weird. Good thing my best buds Joey Gaynor (he's the one with the long hair and a nose ring), Jimmy Pierce (the total brainiac in the porkpie hat), and Gilda Gold (the curly-haired Boston Red Sox fan and comedy film fanatic) are working on the show with me. In fact, Gilda is our director. She's also kind of my girlfriend. Maybe. Don't quote me on that.

"We're back," Mr. Wetmore says through the ceiling speakers in the sound stage. Richard Wetmore is the show's tech director. He's up in the control booth with all the knobs, buttons, and levers. "We're back" means we all need to go back to work. The crew has finished putting together the scenery. The studio audience applauds. They're eager to see us shoot our final scene.

To be honest, it's one I haven't really been looking forward to. Not because the final scene of the final episode means we'll be finished making funny TV shows for the year.

Nope. I'm dreading this scene for another reason.

It takes place at an amusement park. In the Tunnel of Love. You know, one of those romantic rides where you drift down a man-made stream in a dinky dinghy through a very dark passageway.

I might be fine if I were the only one in the scene. But I'm not. I'll be sharing the boat with Donna Dinkle, the Hollywood sitcom star playing Jillda Jewel. Yes, that's the TV version of Gilda Gold.

And guess what the script says we do at the end of the scene, when we come out of the Tunnel of Love?

That's right. We're supposed to kiss.

Chapter 3

SAIL IT WITH A KISS

I'm sweating, of course.

Big surprise.

When you kiss somebody in a TV show, several million total strangers see you do it. So does that studio audience.

"I put on an extra layer of lip gloss," gushes Donna Dinkle.

She looooves the kissy-face scenes the writers are always putting into the *Jamie Funnie* scripts. Me? Not so much.

"It's cotton candy flavor," she whispers. "It kind of goes with the whole carnival feel of the scene. I hope you like it."

I just nod. I'm glad she didn't go with the even more carnival-ish hot-dog-and-pickle-relish-flavored lip goo.

While we're inside the tunnel, a makeup team is supposed to stamp red lipstick smooch marks all over my face. That will make it look like Jillda and I have been kissing the whole time we've been off camera!

It might be fake, but Donna's goo-goo eyes at me aren't.

"You ready to roll, Jamie?" asks Gilda.

"Always," I say as I nudge the wheels of my chair and power up a ramp to the love boat loading dock. When you're the star of the show, you have to work a little harder than everybody else. When you're in a wheelchair, you push yourself even more. Literally. You should see the size of my arm muscles.

Two burly stagehands grab hold of my armrests and hoist me into the boat. Once I'm in place, they secure my wheels to the boat's bottom boards with safety straps.

Donna steps into the boat and sits down on the bench seat.

She's clearly eager to start shooting.

"This reminds me of that ride at Disney World," Donna coos. "It's a Small World."

Then she starts singing that song. The one where the lyrics keep repeating *"It's a small world after all, it's a small, small world."*

Over and over and over. And over and over and over.

"It's a small world—"

Thankfully, Gilda shouts, "Quiet on the set!"

A bell rings.

"Aaaaand, action!"

The boat slides into the tunnel. I forget what I'm supposed to say. I also forget my name and my home address. I forget everything I've ever known, even how to tie my shoes, which is fine because I mostly wear slip-on sneakers these days.

I'm panicking. Fortunately, Donna Dinkle is a pro. She did a ton of sitcoms before we cast her in *Jamie Funnie*. She covers for me by ad-libbing a version of my line. "No, Jamie, I don't wish this were the Tunnel of Tacos."

She snuggles up to my right wheel. The studio audience goes, "Wooooo!" The way they always do right before something mushy happens.

Our love boat glides into the dark tunnel entrance. The audience can't see what we're doing back there. So they keep *woo*ing while the makeup team stamps smooch marks on my face, which isn't easy because my skin is slick with sweat. Ten seconds later, our little boat comes out the other side.

The studio audience cracks up. Because my face is covered with red lip prints.

And Donna's poised to give me one more.

The audience laughs. Donna smacks me—right on

the lips. (It's just about the only empty spot on my face. The makeup artists were very thorough.)

"Awwwww!" The audience swoons. I nearly faint. The parts of my face that aren't already red with lipstick turn pink.

I remember my last line. "*Now* can we go visit the Tunnel of Tacos?"

The audience cracks up. Gilda calls, "Cut! That's a wrap! Good work this year, everybody!"

The audience gives us a standing ovation (something I haven't been able to give myself in years).

Gilda comes over as the crew guys haul me out of the boat.

"You were brilliant, Jamie!" she tells me.

Then she kisses me, too! On the cheek.

Now my face turns purple.

Good thing this picture's in black and white. Otherwise, you'd think I was a grape.

Chapter 4

LOVE IS IN THE AIR.
SO IS MY B.O.

A group of Japanese tourists streams down to the stage after Gilda calls the wrap.

I hope they don't smell how much I've been sweating. One day, I am going to launch my own brand of deodorant: I Sweaty.

Seems being in the studio audience for *Jamie Funnie* was part of the tour group's "Hollywood in New York City" VIP package. Meeting me was part of that package, too.

"We donate all the VIP visit fees to charity," explains Latoya Sherron, a producer on my show.

"Cool," I say. A lot of the money we make on *Jamie*

Funnie goes to the Hope Trust Foundation, which runs the hospital where I went for physical therapy right after the horrible car accident that put me in my chair. The doctors up there studied my case and decided that laughter would be my best medicine. So they kept giving me joke books and classic comedy DVDs.

They saved my life. They also helped make me who I am today. The least I can do is try to give back a little so they can help some other kids in even worse shape than I was.

"You funny!" says the Japanese tour guide, while his group surrounds me on the stage.

"No," I say, "I'm Jamie."

The tour guide does a quick translation.

A dozen of my Japanese fans crack up.

So I pop a wheelie and pull a funny face.

Now they're doubled over with laughter. It's true. Laughter is the universal language. It's something everybody everywhere does the same. And if you do something physically funny, you don't even need a translator. That's probably why Charlie Chaplin, the silent movie comedian, was the biggest movie star the world has ever known.

I pose for selfies, sign a bunch of autographs, do one more funny face, and then head into my dressing room to (finally) wipe off all those smooch marks.

Uncle Frankie is waiting for me. (The real one who twirls yo-yos, not the British actor who plays him on TV.) He sees my lipstick-plastered face and whistles.

"Wow, Jamie. Exactly how many times did Donna Dinkle smooch you when you two were offstage in that tunnel?"

"Just once," I say. "The makeup crew gave me all the other ones."

He nods. "They have the hots for you, too, huh?"

I shake my head and laugh. I know he's joking.

"Say, speaking of love," Uncle Frankie says, kind of randomly, since, technically, we were speaking of kisses, not love. "I have some big news, kiddo."

"You're entering another yo-yo contest?" (When he was younger, Uncle Frankie was a world-class yo-yo champion. Now he calls yo-yos "the original fidget spinners.")

"Nope," he says. "This is even bigger."

"You're adding a triple-decker burger to the diner menu?"

"Bigger still."

"Quadruple-decker? Four meat patties with cheese in between?"

"Nope. Flora and I are getting married! Next weekend!"

Chapter 5

MARRIAGE. IT HAS A NICE RING TO IT.

Flora Denning is the librarian at Long Beach Middle School, where I go when I'm not taping TV shows. She's smart and nice, and I liked her right away.

Not too long ago, my friends and I (with a little nudge from Uncle Frankie) helped Ms. Denning save her library from the scheming principal, who had diabolical plans to turn the heart of the school (that's what a library is) into a sweat room for his wrestling team. He's the *ex*-principal now because of all that scheming and diabolical planning.

"Jamie," says Uncle Frankie, fixing me with a superserious look. "I want you to be my best man."

"B-b-best man? But I'm just a kid. I'm not sure I can, officially, be a man, especially not the *best* one. Isn't that against the rules?"

"Rules, schmules. I want you to stand up for me, Jamie."

I can't resist the comedic softball Uncle Frankie just lobbed my way. "And I'd love to stand up for you, too. Heck, I'd love to stand up for anybody. I'd even love to stand in line at the post office, but the docs tell me it would take a medical miracle."

"You know what I mean, kiddo." Uncle Frankie puts his hand on my shoulder. "This is going to be one of the happiest days of my life. I need you there by my side. Flora wants you to be my best man, too. If it weren't for you…for what you guys did…Flora and I…"

Now he's stammering. His eyes are getting kind of moist. Mine, too.

"I'm in," I say as quickly as I can so neither one of us starts blubbering. "Are you guys going to exchange yo-yos instead of rings?"

"We might, kiddo," Uncle Frankie says with a wink and a smile. "We just might."

Uncle Frankie and Flora are going to make such a happy couple. At the risk of sounding too schmaltzy, they're lucky to have found someone they want to spend the rest of their life with. I wonder if I'll ever get to be that lucky one day.

Eager to spread the happy news, I hurry home to Smileyville, which is what I call my aunt and uncle Kosgrov's place. I call the Kosgrov house Smileyville because none of them ever smile. Not even the dog.

Have Yourself A Miserable Little Christmas!

You know how I said laughter was the universal language? The Smileys never got the memo.

I've been living with the Smileys ever since I moved to Long Beach on Long Island not so long ago. I sleep in the garage, which, by the way, is awesome. There are no steps. I don't even need a ramp. I can just roll up the doors with my remote and roll on in.

Also, I've turned the place into my kid cave, which is kind of like a man cave, only better—with more video game gear, a flat-screen TV, tons of joke books, and a nacho cheese dispenser.

Smileyville is also where my cousin Stevie lives. Stevie Kosgrov.

Maybe you've heard of him. Or seen his face on a wanted poster.

Because Stevie Kosgrov holds the record for being Long Beach Middle School's biggest bully.

And I hold the record for being his biggest target.

Chapter 6

THERE'S A NEW STEVIE IN TOWN

The good news?

My cousin the bully has changed his ways. Ever since we did a comedy team act together at the Hope Trust Children's Rehabilitation Center, he's channeled all his pent-up aggression into protecting me. He's like my live-in bodyguard. The only people he threatens these days are the ones who don't laugh at my jokes.

"Yo, Jamie," he says after politely knocking on the door that connects my garage to the rest of the house.

"What's up, Stevie?"

"Security alert. Mom's making green bean casserole

for dinner." He pounds his fist into the palm of his open hand. "You want I should go have a word with her? Maybe discuss your menu options?"

"No, thanks. I don't mind your mom's green bean casserole."

"It's the one with the cream of mushroom soup and burnt cornflake crumbs on top."

"It's fine, Stevie."

"You sure?"

"Positive."

Stevie pulls out a little notebook and licks the tip of a stubby pencil. "Anybody give you grief on the set today?"

"Nope. No problems on the set."

"How about that Donna Dingle? She can be a real pain in the patootie."

"She was fine."

"And Joe Amodio, your big-shot producer?"

"He's fine, too," I tell Stevie. "In fact, our final episode is in the can. We wrapped for the season."

"You guys did a rap? In the can? Was there toilets involved?"

"Sure," I say.

Because it's easier.

That night, over dinner, I tell the Smileys what I know about Uncle Frankie's upcoming wedding.

"The service will be next Saturday at the church. The reception will be at the diner with a full burger and meat loaf buffet. Instead of gifts, they want everybody to donate a book to the middle school library."

The Smileys nod. They do not smile.

"I'm sure it will be a very emotional wedding," I

say. "I bet even the cake will be in tiers."

Silence. Guess they forgot that *tiers* are what you call the layers in a layer cake.

So I try a few more wedding zingers.

"When the TV repairman got married, I hear the reception was amazing. Hey, do you know what they call a melon that's not allowed to marry? A cantaloupe."

I tug at my collar. I'm bombing. Again.

Stevie squints at his family.

"Laugh, people!" he bellows.

"Why?" asks his little brother. "Did somebody fart?"

Nobody chuckles. Except, of course, me.

Stevie sighs and shakes his head. "Sorry, Jamie. These people are impossible."

"Nah," I say. "These people are my family."

When I say that, Aunt Smiley doesn't laugh.

But she does smile.

Me too.

Chapter 7

THE PLANET'S FUNNIEST KID COMIC, VERSION 2.0

That weekend, I head to Radio City Music Hall in New York City to host the Second Annual Planet's Funniest Kid Comic competition.

That's the contest I won last year. That means I'll be turning over my crown to a new kid comic tonight.

Uncle Frankie and his fiancée come into the city with me. We arrive in the souped-up limo-van that Joe Amodio sent out to Long Island to pick us up. It's *very* wheelchair-accessible. We're talking hydraulic lifts.

"Will this year's winner get their own TV show, too?" asks Ms. Denning.

Gulp. Did not think of that.

Is Joe Amodio, the producer of the Planet's Funniest Kid Comic Contest and *Jamie Funnie*, looking to replace me?

"If they do get their own show," says Uncle Frankie, "it'll never be as funny as Jamie's."

"Thanks," I say.

Uncle Frankie shrugs. "Hey, how could it be? Their show wouldn't have an Uncle Frankie in it."

He sees the look on my face. I'm giving him my sad puppy dog eyes.

"I'm kidding, Jamie. What the new kid's show would be missing is *you*!"

He claps me on the back and we head through the stage door. Jacky Hart, from *Saturday Night Live*, is in the hallway with her daughters, Tina and Grace. Jacky Ha-Ha (that's what everybody called her when she was my age) is going to be my cohost for the live broadcast of the kid comedy competition.

"Hiya, Jamie," she says.

Her daughters squeal. "Jamie!"

What can I say? They're big fans. Grace wants me to autograph her forehead. Tina wants me to sign her shoe. I do.

Joe Amodio, the big-time TV producer, strolls up the hallway.

"There they are! My two favorite funny people!"

"You mean Grace and Tina?" I say. They giggle. Mr. Amodio slaps me on the back.

"Kid, you still crack me up. Seriously, Jamie. You do. But this year's competition? Tonight's just the start."

"I thought these were the finals," says Jacky.

"They are," says Mr. Amodio.

Then he winks.

"For the *USA* competition. Whoever wins tonight? They're moving on to the brand-new, superexciting international round. And guess what, Jamie?"

"What?"

"You're going with them!"

An international competition where nobody understands a single word I'm saying? Sheesh. Welcome back to my United Nations nightmare.

Chapter 8

IT'S NEWS TO ME

Mr. Amodio flicks his wrist to check his watch. It's one of those sleek ones that count your steps. That's why I'll never own one.

"We'll talk, *bubelah*," he says with a grin. "But the big international competition won't start for a few weeks. Right now, I need you to focus on being funny and hosting this new crop of kids."

"B-b-but…" I stammer.

"Is that your new Porky Pig impersonation?" asks Mr. Amodio. "I love it, Jamie. *Love. It.* But don't use it in the show, *capisce?* Copyright issues. Jacky? You ready to rock?"

"Tartar sauce!" she says. "Barnacles!"

"No SpongeBob catchphrases, either!" shouts Mr. Amodio. "You two jokers. You slay me. Seriously.

You do." He walks away, chuckling and shaking his head. "Comedians. Can't live with 'em. Can't lock 'em in a bathroom."

"See you out there, Jamie," says Jacky, ducking into her dressing room. "Come on, guys. Mom has to put on her clown suit."

"You're wearing a clown suit?" asks Grace.

"Will you give us balloons?" asks Tina.

"It's just an expression," I hear Jacky say as the dressing room door closes.

When they're gone, Ms. Denning looks at me with a goofy grin. Then she starts clapping her hands together. "This is so exciting, Jamie. You might be in another competition! You might get to travel to another country!"

"This is the first I've heard about it."

"I'll try to buttonhole Mr. Amodio," says Uncle Frankie. "Find out what the heck he's talking about."

"I don't want to compete again," I say, feeling the butterflies dancing the cha-cha in my stomach.

"Don't worry, Jamie," says Uncle Frankie, placing his hands on my shoulders to steady me. "Keep calm and carry on."

"That's what the British say."

"I know. Nigel Bigglebottom taught it to me. Now go out there, have fun, and host the best show you've ever hosted."

I nod. I'm going to try.

"And," says Ms. Denning, "if you do get nervous, just think about how petrified all the kids in the competition must feel."

She's right. I've been there, done that, have the sweat-soaked T-shirt to prove it. I am *sooooo* glad I'm not one of the dozen kid comics vying to be this year's funniest kid on the planet.

A production assistant comes over and hands me a stack of note cards.

"Hiya, Jamie," she says. "Here's the info on the kids you'll be introducing. You'll do these six, Jacky will do the other six. Feel free to ad-lib if you don't love the jokes the writers came up with."

"Thanks," I tell her.

I look down at the cards and see the names of all the kids who want to take my place as the funniest kid on the planet.

And if Mr. Amodio is thinking what I think he's thinking, one of them might get a chance to defeat me, too.

Chapter 9

THE NEW KIDS ON THE BLOCK

The Planet's Funniest Kid Comic Finals is a live TV show.

That means I need to stay focused. I should be used to performing for an audience, but even after filming *Jamie Funnie* for months in front of people, I still get nervous. Every. Single. Time. So I try to forget whatever Mr. Amodio might've said about me competing in some kind of new international contest.

The jokes the staff writers whipped up for my contestant intros are probably pretty good. But I can't read the note cards. My flop sweat has now dribbled down from my forehead and into my eyeballs.

Jacky and I improvise a quick bit to open the show.

"Well, Jamie," says Jacky, "tonight's the big night. One of these twelve contestants will be crowned the new funniest kid on this planet."

"Yes," I say. "My reign as champion of the planet is nearing an end."

Jacky nods. "I think that means you have to move to Mars."

The audience laughs.

"Is Mars one of those planets with zero gravity?" I

37

ask, looking up from my wheelchair. "Because float-ing would be a whole lot easier than pumping rubber all day!"

Another laugh.

Jacky introduces our first comic, who calls him-self Don Pickles. I think it's a stage name. He's a scowling fifth grader in a shiny leopard-print jacket doing a furious version of the legendary insult com-edian Don Rickles's schtick. He starts prowling the stage, working the audience.

"That's a nice jacket you're wearing, sir," he says to a man in a plaid sport coat. "Go pick up some cot-ton candy on your way home and join the circus." He moves down the first row of seats. "I don't know this gentleman in the beard. Good luck in Bethlehem, sir. I have a friend who said an onion is the only food that can make you cry. So I threw a coconut at his face. At school, they taught us that light trav-els faster than sound. That's why some people seem bright until you hear them speak."

Don Pickles is a little, um, angry for my taste. In my act, I try to have fun without making fun of other people. Even if I'm competing against them in some kind of new international contest that Joe Amodio just dreamed up.

Ooops.

I wasn't supposed to be thinking about that, was I?

Guess that's why I just missed my entrance cue!

Chapter 10

THE CORNBALL QUEEN

"*Pssst!* Jamie?"

The stage manager snaps me out of my sweat-soaked, panic-streaked trance.

"You're on!"

I wipe my forehead with a polka-dotted handkerchief and roll onstage to my microphone.

"Ladies and gentlemen," I say, "our next comedian needs no introduction. So what am I doing out here? Well, the brake on my chair doesn't work so I just sort of rolled onstage. I'm kidding. I wouldn't miss this next comedian's set for all the cheese at Chuck E.'s. I give you the one, the only...Conor Cronin!"

The audience cheers. Conor Cronin cradles the microphone at center stage and sort of mumbles into it.

"I went to a customer information booth at the mall," drones Conor Cronin in a deadpan monotone as he recycles some of Steven Wright's best lines. "I asked them to tell me about some of the people who shopped there last week. There was a power outage at the mall while I was there. At least two dozen people were trapped on the escalators. Just remember—everywhere is walking distance if you have the time, but on the other hand...you have different fingers."

Jacky introduces the next comic, a guy named Mick Shaffer, who makes jokes while juggling stuff—including toasters and Pop Tarts. Then there's Tom Carrozza, a ventriloquist, and Kim Sykes, who does celebrity impersonations.

We work our way through half a dozen more comics, all of them very funny. I introduce the final act: ten-year-old Grace Garner from Cedar Falls, Iowa. She's extremely cute and calls herself the Corn Queen—and not just because she's from Iowa. She has some of the corniest two-liners I've ever heard. But she tells them with such conviction and such incredible timing (not to mention a dimpled grin) that she's hysterical and unbelievably adorable!

"Do you know where bees go to the bathroom? The nearest BP station. What's brown and has a head and tail but no legs? A penny! You know why the banana went to the hospital? It wasn't peeling very well."

She reels them off, one after another, with the rat-a-tat-tat speed of a laser cannon in a Star Wars video game.

When all the votes are tallied, we have a winner.

Yep. Grace Garner. America loves its corn. Especially when it's popped up hot and fast and sweet.

"Perfect!" says Joe Amodio when we're off the air. "You and Grace are gonna be great together."

"Um, when?"

"We'll talk."

And I thought that was what we *were* doing.

"Swing by the office tomorrow with Frankie, kid. We'll do lunch. And, Jamie?"

"Yes, sir?"

"This is going to be huge! The hugest thing we've ever done together!"

Chapter 11

SOMETHING'S FISHY

Since school and *Jamie Funnie* are both on hiatus for the summer, I head down the boardwalk to Uncle Frankie's diner to grab breakfast.

Good Eats by the Sea is a strange name for a place that serves breakfast, because we Americans don't eat much seafood early in the morning. Nobody ever goes into Burger King and orders an egg and shrimp Croissan'wich. Nobody pulls up to the drive-thru at McDonald's and orders an Egg McMackerel with a side of seaweed.

But according to Uncle Frankie, who studies food (and yo-yos) the way I study comedy, people *do* eat fish for breakfast all the time in Japan. Sweden, too. Probably because neither country has discovered bacon yet.

Ms. Denning and Uncle Frankie are sitting in a booth when I roll through the front door. They're reading some kind of book, which they immediately hide when they see me coming. Because *that's* not suspicious at all.

"Jamie!" says Uncle Frankie. "Pull up a chair."

"No, thanks," I say. "I'll stick with this one. Better padding."

I park my wheelchair perpendicular to the booth.

"You want pancakes?" asks Uncle Frankie.

"French toast?" asks Ms. Denning. "How about a waffle?"

"Sure," I say.

"You want me to make a smiley face on the pancakes with bananas and chocolate chips?"

"Um, I'm not six, Uncle Frankie..."

"Right. So, you don't want the chocolate chips?"

"Of course I do. I just wanted to remind you guys that I graduated kindergarten years ago."

Uncle Frankie whips up a huge platter of pancakes, French toast, waffles, eggs, bacon, and sausage—all of it decorated to the max with sliced fruit, chocolate chips, and Reese's Pieces.

"So, uh, what's going on?" I ask.

Uncle Frankie and Ms. Denning look at each other. He nods.

"Well, Jamie, as you know, your uncle and I are going to get married on Saturday," says Ms. Denning.

I hold my knife to the stack of pancakes. But I can't cut them. Not with Uncle Frankie and Ms. Denning smiling at me like that. I put down my silverware and say, "Right."

Ms. Denning takes Uncle Frankie's hand.

"We're going to be a family," she says.

"Flora and Frankie," says Uncle Frankie. "Frankie and Flora."

Wow. He sounds like he's more nervous than I was right before I rolled onstage at my very first comedy competition in Ronkonkoma.

"You tell him, Frankie," says Ms. Denning.

"You sure, hon?"

"I can't. It makes me too happy."

She's all choked up and dabbing at her eyes with a paper napkin.

Okay now. What is going on?

"Well, Jamie," says Frankie. "As you know, you've been my nephew for a long time. Ever since you were born. And I've been your uncle. Which is why you call me Uncle Frankie."

I'm pretty sure he'll get to the point. Eventually.

Now Uncle Frankie honks his nose in a napkin and sniffles back some tears.

"Jamie, I know I can't ever replace your dad... my baby brother..."

"And I'll never replace your mother," says Ms. Denning. "Nobody can."

"But," says Uncle Frankie, "now that Flora and I are, like we said, going to be a family and all, we think it would be an even better family if *you* came along for the ride."

I nod slowly. I'm not exactly sure what he's talking about.

Then I look down at the booth bench and see the book they hid when I first rolled into the diner:

THINGS I DID NOT SEE COMING

Whoa!

It's like Uncle Frankie and Ms. Denning are proposing to me. They want to become my adoptive parents.

"Could I still live in a garage?" I ask.

"Whatever you want, kiddo!" says Uncle Frankie.

"We just want to share the rest of our lives with you," says his bride-to-be.

"Officially," adds Uncle Frankie.

"Do you think the Smileys will mind?" I say. "They've been awfully good to me."

(Except for the part about having a psycho-bully son named Stevie, but even that's sort of worked itself out.)

"I talked to your aunt and uncle," says Frankie. "The Kosgrovs think it would be a wonderful idea."

"Well, then," I say with a smile wider than the one on my waffle, "so do I!"

And then we all hug. And sniffle. And sob.

Like Uncle Frankie and Flora said, no one could ever replace my mom and dad and sister, but this is the next-best thing. I'll have my own family again.

There's nothing more important than that.

After we talk about a few details, I devour my breakfast platter because Uncle Frankie and I have to hurry into New York City for that lunch meeting with Joe Amodio. (Yes, I might gain fifteen pounds in one day.) Gilda joins us.

If it has anything to do with *Jamie Funnie* or just Jamie Grimm, I definitely want Gilda in my corner!

"Jamie! Frankie! Gilda!"

Mr. Amodio is all open arms and smiles when we enter his office on the forty-third floor of the BNC Tower in midtown Manhattan. The guy has a great view of the city. And a telescope parked near the windows.

"So glad you guys could join us today," he says.

"Us?" says Uncle Frankie, arching an eyebrow.

"I think he's using the royal *we*," says Gilda.

"I could," says Mr. Amodio, puffing up his chest. "And I usually do. But not today. Come on. The gang's waiting for us in my conference room."

"The gang?" I say.

"A consortium of TV producers from around the world. We've got folks from Germany, Brazil, Australia, Kenya, Russia, the United Arab Emirates, Sweden, Japan…"

"Did they eat fish for breakfast this morning?" I ask.

"Huh?"

"Never mind."

Mr. Amodio chuckles. "You crack me up, kid. Seriously, you do. Even when I don't know what the heck you're talking about, you make me laugh. Come on. Let's go meet our new international partners!"

He opens the sliding doors and we enter the conference room. Very serious men and women in business suits are gathered around a huge table. Uncle Frankie is tugging at the untucked tails of his Hawaiian-print shirt, probably wishing he'd worn something different or at least put on a tie.

I have the feeling that, unlike the meeting I had with Uncle Frankie and Aunt Flora, this one isn't going to end in big hugs.

Chapter 13

GLOBAL FREEZING

"**J**amie, baby," says Mr. Amodio. "Let me cut to the chase. The Planet's Funniest Kid Comic competition has been a *huge* success here in the good old US of A. Well, now it's time to share the wealth with the rest of the world. Because, hey—how can you be the funniest kid on the planet if most of that planet wasn't even represented in the competition, am I right?"

"This is true!" says a businessman who sounds a lot like Mr. Burdzecki, a customer at Uncle Frankie's diner who came from Russia when it used to be the Soviet Union.

The Russian guy growls at me. "We wish to challenge you, the so-called number one funny boy of the world. We have funny boy. His name is Vasily. He will bury you."

"But, um, Grace Garner is the new American champion, not me," I say as sweat trickles down my spine. I hate when it does that.

"True," says Mr. Amodio. "That's why Grace Garner is going to join you on Team USA at the finals."

"Uh, what finals are we talking about here?"

"Zee finals for zee new worldwide competition!" says a man with a thick accent.

"These are going to be the Olympics of Comedy, Jamie," says Mr. Amodio. "First, you host a series of regional competitions. The Americas. Australia. Africa. Asia. The Middle East. Europe."

Uncle Frankie whistles. "You're gonna rack up a ton of frequent flyer miles, kiddo."

"You're gonna need a bigger suitcase," adds Gilda.

I'm also gonna need better antiperspirant.

"Jamie," says Mr. Amodio, "my colleagues have flown in from all over the world…"

"And boy, are their arms tired," I say. It's a reflex. Toss me a classic setup, I'll counter with its punch line. But nobody laughs. Instead, everybody stares, glares, and glowers. And then they explode.

I don't understand a word they're screaming.

Except for the Australian dude. He speaks English. Sort of.

When they're done screaming at me, they start screaming at one another.

"Germans have no sense of humor!" shouts the Russian.

"Oh, yes we do!" hollers the German. "We laugh at Russia all the time!"

"You people eat yeast!" the Brazilian yells at the Australian.

"It's called Vegemite, mate. And it's a ripper. Makes us funnier than a kangaroo playin' a didgeridoo!"

Uncle Frankie stands up and grabs hold of my chair's handles. "We're outta here," he says. "Come on, Gilda. Give me a call, Joe, when you knuckleheads stop screaming at each other and hash this thing out."

And then he pushes me out of the room.

Usually, I don't like it when somebody drives me around like a suitcase with wheels.

But right now? I love it. Because Uncle Frankie can shove me out of that room faster than I could've shoved myself.

Chapter 14

STUMP THE JOKESTER

Looking for a little normalcy, I work the dinner rush at Uncle Frankie's diner.

It's kind of where my whole comedy career got started. Before I ever entered my first young comedian contest, Uncle Frankie let me man the cash register at Good Eats by the Sea and ring up a classic joke for any customer who requested one.

With time, it's turned into a bit like the "Stump the Band" routine that the late, great Johnny Carson used to do when he hosted *The Tonight Show* (they had *all* his DVDs at the Hope Trust Children's Rehabilitation Center).

Some of Uncle Frankie's regulars even try to trip me up by asking for comics they think nobody my age has ever heard of. But I have yet to be thrown. I've heard of and studied them all.

"Phyllis Diller," says Mrs. Mankowitz with a sly "gotcha" grin as she hands me her dinner check and a twenty-dollar bill. Phyllis Diller was big back in the 1960s, waaaay before I was born. But that doesn't mean I don't know her jokes.

"We spend the first twelve months of our children's lives teaching them to walk and talk," I say, firing off one of Diller's best one-liners, "and the next twelve years teaching them to sit down and shut up."

I give myself a BADA-BING with the cash register keys and hand Mrs. Mankowitz her change.

Next up is a guy who loves George Carlin jokes. I give him a daily double. "If a pig loses its voice, is it disgruntled? Remember—don't sweat the petty things and don't pet the sweaty things."

"Here's one you won't know," says a lady with a very proper British accent. "Peter Kay!"

Ooh. I'm impressed. Peter Kay is high on the obscure-comic scale. At least here in America. He's actually very big around the world. In fact, this English comedian's 2010–2011 stand-up tour made it into *Guinness World Records* as the most successful of all time, playing to more than 1.2 million people!

And yes, I've memorized a few of his best jokes, including the one I tell the lady with the English accent.

"My dad used to say 'always fight fire with fire.' Which is probably why he got thrown out of the fire brigade."

From the early-bird specials to the late dinner crowd, I keep it up. Nobody stumps me.

Steven Wright: "I think it's wrong that only one company makes the game Monopoly."

Bada-bing!

Groucho Marx: "I never forget a face, but in your case I'd be glad to make an exception."

Lily Tomlin: "The trouble with the rat race is that, even if you win, you're still a rat."

When things finally calm down, Uncle Frankie gestures for me to join him in the kitchen. This is where we've had a lot of our very important uncle-to-nephew chats. He sits on a pickle barrel. I park near a stack of canned corn.

"I've got some big news," says Uncle Frankie.

Suddenly, I feel like the corn. I'm all ears.

Chapter 15

INTERNATIONAL INTRIGUE

"**M**r. Amodio just called," says Uncle Frankie.

He pulls a wrinkled sheet of paper out of his pocket. On one side is a grocery list. On the other, notes from his telephone conversation with Mr. Amodio.

"He and the rest of those assorted international knuckleheads finally hashed out the details for this international Planet's Funniest Kid Comic dealio. You'd be the host for a series of televised regional finals we'd do in South America, Asia, Australia, Africa, the Middle East, and Europe."

"How do the comics make it to the finals?" I ask.

"Video submissions over the internet. Folks would vote for their favorites online. The shows you'd be hosting would feature the best of the best and would shoot in Rio de Janeiro, Tokyo, Sydney, Nairobi, Dubai, and Berlin. One right after the other."

"So I'd be going around the world in eighty days?"

"More like three weeks. I'm getting jet lag just thinking about it."

Sheesh. Might as well fly to the moon while we're at it.

Uncle Frankie checks his notes.

"Get this. The official rules state that all the jokes in the regional finals must be delivered in English."

"Really?" I say. "That sounds extremely unfair."

"I know. But Mr. Amodio says it's the only way to sell the show to an American television audience.

We don't know as many foreign languages as they do over in Europe, where everybody knows two or three different ones."

I gulp a little. Because every chance to steal the show is also an opportunity to fall flat on my face, which in my case usually involves some wheelchair tipping.

"So these regional shows will be broadcast here at home?" I ask.

Uncle Frankie nods. "The big finals in London, too. Those will be like the Olympics. The top kid comics from each region will compete for the title of Planet's Funniest Kid Comic Worldwide. That's the round you're supposed to compete in, kiddo. You and Grace Garner, the cornball from Iowa."

Uncle Frankie stands up and puts his hand on my shoulder.

"I know you're not keen on competing again, but, well, it might be fun. Plus, you'd get to see the world. Sleep on it. Mr. Amodio needs an answer by Monday morning. We'll talk more about it after the thing tomorrow."

I nod.

But then I have to ask.

"What thing tomorrow?"

Uncle Frankie gives me a funny look. "Nothing too important. Only my wedding, Mr. Best Man."

I actually slap my forehead and say, "Doh!"

Uncle Frankie laughs. "You know, Jamie, not for nothing, but the best man's most important job is to make sure the groom gets to the church on time. Remembering when the wedding is taking place might be a good start."

"Gotcha. So, uh, what's my second-most-important job?"

"Making a toast and giving a speech at the reception."

I have to make a speech?

Guess I'm going to have to change my underwear again. Because all of a sudden, flop sweat is trickling down my spine like crazy!

Chapter 16

A WONDERFULLY WACKY WEDDING

Uncle Frankie and New Aunt Flora's wedding is beautiful.

And yes, we make it to the church on time. I even wear a tuxedo. I'm also in charge of hanging on to the official ring Uncle Frankie slips on Ms. Denning's finger. He keeps the unofficial yo-yo hidden in *his* tux pocket. It's a Duncan Pulse. The kind that lights up when it twirls. Ms. Denning surprises Uncle Frankie by giving him a yo-yo, too! Hers whistles when it unwinds.

Like I said, the wedding is beautiful and just a little wacky.

What goes
BUZZZZZ, ZZZZZUB,
BUZZZZZ, ZZZZZUB?
A bee stuck to a yo-yo.

After Uncle Frankie and Ms. Denning are officially pronounced "husband and wife" (which, if you ask me, is a funny way to pronounce their names), we all hurry back to the diner for the reception.

The Smileys headed up the decoration committee, and the place looks spectacular. There's all sorts of curling white crepe-paper streamers and a ton of those fold-out honeycomb wedding bells hanging off the ceiling. The delicious aromas of hamburgers and meat loaf waft in the air.

I've worked on my best man toast and have it tucked inside my tuxedo jacket.

Gilda is sort of my date for the wedding. Not that we're on a date. We're just both wearing fancy clothes and we arrived together in the same vehicle so, yeah, I can see how people might think it was a date.

"Nervous about making your toast?" she asks.

"A little bit," I confess.

"Don't worry," she says, combing a stray strand of hair out of my eyes. "You're a pro, Jamie. Saying witty stuff in front of a whole bunch of people is what you do."

"But this is special."

"I agree," says Gilda. Then she looks at me with what can only be described as goo-goo eyes. "You know, Jamie, I think it's awesome when two people who were meant to be together forever find each other."

"Yeah," I say.

Gilda's eyes widen. Then they start blinking. Repeatedly.

"And," says Gilda, "I think it's even more awesome when those two people find each other *early* in life. Maybe even when they're in middle school."

I think I know where she's going with this, so I do what I usually do when I panic. I crack a joke. "I guess that's why they say the early bird gets the worm. But the second mouse gets the cheese!"

Gilda quits making goo-goo eyes so she can roll them at me.

I'm saved by the bell. Actually, it's somebody dinging a fork against the side of a glass, but it sounds like a bell. It's time for the toasts.

I'm on!

Chapter 17

TOAST WITH JAM

"Ladies and gentlemen!" I say, holding up my glass of lemon-lime soda. "As best man, or in my case, best kid, I'd like to say a few words."

"Hear, hear!" shouts one of Frankie's regulars.

"Yes, sir. Right here is where I plan on doing it. As you guys know, I've studied a lot of classic comedians. Many of them had a lot to say about love and marriage. For instance, Rodney Dangerfield. He said, 'My wife and I were happy for twenty years. Then we met.'"

People laugh.

"I don't know much about marriage, being in middle school and all, but I like Rita Rudner's take on it: 'I love being married. It's so great to find one special person you want to annoy for the rest of your life!'"

More laughs.

"I'm joking because I think humor is important in a marriage. So is a very short memory."

I raise my glass a little higher.

There's no joking about this. Uncle Frankie? Aunt Flora? You two are lucky you found each other. And so are all of us!

"May your 'for better or for worse' always be far better than it is worse."

Everybody raises their glasses and cheers.

Uncle Frankie dances the first dance with Aunt Flora. I see Aunt Smiley sniffling back a tear. Stevie Kosgrov, too.

People start dancing to the doo-wop music tumbling out of the diner's jukebox. Well, everybody except me. I really don't have the moves anymore.

Gilda thinks otherwise.

"Come on, Jamie," she says. "Let's dance."

"Um, I think you're supposed to use your legs when you do that..."

Gilda grins. "You ever been to a Jewish wedding?"

"No."

"They do a chair dance called the hora. I think we should do it, too."

And that's how I end up being hoisted into the air in my chair by Gaynor, Pierce, Mr. Burdzecki, and Uncle Frankie, next to Gilda in her chair, being held up by Stevie and the entire Kosgrov family.

When they put me back on the floor, I keep on jamming. I pop a few wheelies, do some spins, and shimmy my tires to the beat. Pretty soon, other people grab chairs and try to match my moves. It's like we just invented our own Chicken Dance, but with chairs.

It's pretty hysterical.

"Thanks," I tell Gilda.

"For what?"

"Helping me remember I can have just as much fun as anybody else. I just have to work a little harder for it!"

After the cake is cut and Aunt Flora tosses her

bouquet over her shoulder, Uncle Frankie motions for me to join him in his "office."

Yep. We're back in the kitchen. He's on the pickle barrel, I'm in my chair.

Uncle Frankie has a very serious look on his face.

I think we're about to have another very important uncle-nephew chat.

Either that, or he ate too many pickles.

Chapter 18

DEEP THINKING NEAR THE DEEP FRYER

"**F**lora and I are about to take off," he tells me.

"Where are you guys going on your honeymoon?" I ask.

"Niagara Falls. We're old-school."

"Don't go over it in a barrel."

"Not on the itinerary. But, Jamie?"

"Yeah?"

"Speaking of itineraries, I've been thinking. If you say yes to this international comedy contest, maybe Flora and I could go with you. As your, you know, chaperones."

I nod. Hey, I'm still a kid. Nobody would let me fly around the world as an unaccompanied minor.

"I could ask my weekend guy, Vinnie, to mind the diner while we're gone," says Frankie. "Flora has the whole summer off from school. We'd be there to look out for you. Make sure Mr. Amodio doesn't make you do something you don't want to."

"I'd appreciate that," I say.

"It's your call, kiddo. But, well, if the three of us do this trip around the world together, it might help us all get a head start on building our new family. I want you and Flora to get to know each other better."

What Uncle Frankie's saying makes a lot of sense.

But it also makes me a little squeamish. If I do the worldwide tour, I don't just have to emcee a bunch of shows all over the world. I also have to go to London and compete in the finals. Making plans with Uncle Frankie makes it feel like I'm really doing it.

Even though I'm not sure I want to.

"Think about it," Uncle Frankie says. "Flora and I will be fine either way."

"But it'd be a nice second honeymoon for you guys," I say.

"That's not why you should agree to do it. But if you do, I think it'd be good for all of us, Jamie. Our whole brand-new family."

Uncle Frankie and Aunt Flora take off in Uncle Frankie's cherry-red Mustang. Somebody soaped JUST MARRIED on the windows and tied yo-yos to the bumper.

Uncle Frankie gives me a huge grin as he pulls away, and Aunt Flora blows me a kiss.

"See you in a few days, Jamie!" he hollers.

When almost everybody is gone, I help the cleanup crew. Gilda pitches in, too. A few of those white paper wedding bells got knocked off the ceiling during our chair dance.

When the diner's clean, I say good night to Gilda. She gives me a very warm smile.

"I had a wonderful time, Jamie," she says.

"Yeah," I tell her. "Me too."

And then she leaves.

I probably should've kissed her good night. But I'm too busy thinking about stuff.

Like the comedy contest and whether I want to go through all that again.

Would I be happier if I said no to the international tour, quit doing *Jamie Funnie*, and went to live a quiet, non-showbiz life with Uncle Frankie and Aunt Flora? If I did, I could go to school all year like a normal kid. I could live my life out of the spotlight. I could have dinner every night with people who actually get me *and* my jokes. And wouldn't boo me when I was done telling them. Probably.

I roll home to think it over.

I click on my computer and start aimlessly browsing around. I do some of my best ruminating that way. (That's a fancy way of saying cogitating.)

The message icon on my desktop dings.

It's from Gilda.

U need to see this.

There's a link to a video. I click on it.

"As you see, my English is very, very good," says a kid about my age with a thick Russian accent. "So I will do very, very well in this upcoming comedy competition, all the way to the finals in London."

There's a title on the bottom of the screen identifying the boy as Vasily Vasilovich.

Vasily.

That's the kid comic the Russian producer was bragging about in Mr. Amodio's office.

Vasily stares directly into the camera lens. It's almost as if he knows I'm watching.

"As for Jamie Greem? He not funny. In America, he win seeempathy vote. Boo-hoo. Everybody feel so sorry for him. Boo-hoo-hoo. He is in wheelchair. We must give him trophy. Ha! If he enters this new competition, I will crush him *and* his wheelchair."

He's going for my weak spot. The fear that all my success has been built on one thing: sympathy. People feel sorry for me, so they vote for me.

To be honest, I'm tired of hearing that.

So I guess I have to (once again) prove all the Vasilys in the world wrong.

I take a deep breath. Make up my mind. (It's always better to do that with a full tank of oxygen in your lungs.)

I'm calling Joe Amodio first thing Monday.

I'm going to go around the world with Uncle Frankie and Aunt Flora and, hopefully, go up against Vasily Vasilovich at the finals in London, where I will prove, once and for all, that…I Funny!

The Planet's Funniest Kid Comic Worldwide contest?

I'm not only in it.

I'm in it to *win* it!

Chapter 19

LOOK OUT, WORLD, HERE WE COME!

I don't wait until Monday.

I call Mr. Amodio first thing *Sunday* morning.

"I'm in, sir."

"Great, kid," he says. "Wonderful. Couldn't be happier. Quick question?"

"Yes, sir?"

"Do you call a lot of people at six o'clock on a Sunday morning?"

"Only when I'm pumped and stoked, sir."

Since Uncle Frankie and Aunt Flora are still honeymooning up at Niagara Falls on Monday, Gilda comes with me to Mr. Amodio's office so we can hash out the details of the tour.

"Jamie's uncle Frankie and aunt Flora will be his official chaperones," she says. "Mine, too."

"Excuse me?" says Mr. Amodio.

"I'm going with Jamie."

Gilda gives Mr. Amodio her steely, determined look. Nobody ever says no to it.

"Fine," says Mr. Amodio, smoothing down his suit lapels. "Any other demands?"

"Yes. Gaynor and Pierce come with us, too," she says. "I'll be bringing my camera. We might be able to grab some awesome 'on location' footage to cut into next year's episodes of *Jamie Funnie*."

"Sweet," says Mr. Amodio. "I like the way you think, Gilda."

"Yeah," I say. "Me too."

Mr. Amodio starts making a list.

"So that's Jamie, Gilda, Frankie, Flora, Gaynor, and Pierce."

"And Stevie," I say.

"Who?"

"Stevie Kosgrov."

"Seriously, Jamie?" says Gilda. "You want to invite that big blowhard of a bully to go on a trip around the world with you? Did you forget that he's been picking on you ever since you moved to Long Beach?"

"He's changed," I say. "Plus, if this tour is all about everybody in the world sharing a good laugh…"

"Who said it was about that?" says Mr. Amodio. "It's a competition, Jamie. A contest. There's gonna be conflict and tension. Winners and losers."

I don't like the sound of that. "But—"

"If things are going to get nasty," says Gilda, sort of cutting me off, "Jamie's right. He needs Stevie Kosgrov for muscle and protection."

"Fine," says Mr. Amodio, adding Stevie's name to his list. "The bully can come, but that's it."

"Deal," says Gilda.

I still want to say something about the tour promoting world harmony through humor, but Gilda and Mr. Amodio have moved on to travel arrangements.

"Since there's going to be seven of you, we'll charter a private jet. We'll call it Air Funny One."

"Cool!" I say, because, I've got to be honest, flying around the world in my own private jet sounds superawesome.

"It's a win-win," says Mr. Amodio with a shrug. "You kids will be more comfortable. I'll have more control over your movements. Plus, I'm gonna add a few more members to the security team. They'll fly with you guys, too."

"Do we really need extra security guards?" I ask nervously.

"If this show goes the way I hope it will, you sure will, Jamie baby. You know, there's a reason comedians call them punch lines and gags and gut-busters. Done right, comedy is like football or boxing or any other violent sport."

Really?

Too bad. Because I don't want to hurt anybody. I just want to make them laugh!

Chapter 20

PINNING DOWN OUR PLANS

I'm all ready to protest, but once again, I'm cut off.

Mr. Amodio is spinning a globe and sticking pins in it. I hope it's not a voodoo globe.

"First stop will be Rio de Janeiro," he says, poking a red pin into South America.

"The one in Brazil?" says Gilda, with a big smile on her face.

"No, the one in New Jersey," snaps Mr. Amodio. "Of course the one in Brazil. Work with me, Gilda. This is a worldwide competition, remember? That means you're going *around the world*. After Rio, you guys will hit Sydney—the city in Australia, not my accountant. From Australia, you fly up to Tokyo."

He jabs in more pins and gives the globe a spin.

"After Japan, you head to Africa. Nairobi, Kenya. Comedy is big in Kenya these days. Huge! After Nairobi, you'll bop up to Dubai in the United Arab Emirates. Pack your shorts for that stop, folks. Average summertime temp? We're talking one hundred and three, one hundred and six. But it's a dry heat."

Good, I think. *It can dry up all my flop sweat.*

"After Dubai, you head north to Berlin for the European regional round. Last stop: London. For the live finals."

"You'll be our master of ceremonies for the regional stops, Jamie," says Mr. Amodio. "But in London, you hop back into the ring with Team USA to go joke-to-joke against the top two comics from each of the six regions. It'll be a dozen of the funniest kids on the planet against Jamie Grimm and What's-Her-Name."

"Grace Garner," I remind him. "From Iowa."

"I don't care where she's from, *bubelah*. I just care about where you and she are going. To the top. Or maybe the bottom. Either way, it doesn't matter as long as it has drama, suspense, and hopefully some nice hostile conflict. You give me that, you give me what I want more than anything in the world."

"More pins?"

"Nope. Ratings. Big, enormous, must-see-TV ratings!"

"When do we leave?" asks Gilda.

"A week from today."

I really don't like Joe Amodio's idea of pitting us against one another, but this isn't the first time I've heard his thirst for turmoil. He's the creator of *Jamie Funnie*, after all, and asks us to put as

90

much crisis in each episode as we can. But as the director and main character, Gilda and I make sure that any drama is there for a reason, and that it's balanced out with lots of humor.

That gives me an idea. As emcee, and with Gilda with me, I can steer these contests into being friendly competitions instead of comedy death matches!

Besides, comedy should be about making jokes and friends, not insults and enemies.

Gilda and I race back to Long Beach and give Gaynor and Pierce the good news.

"You guys are coming on an all-expenses-paid trip with us around the world!" I tell them.

"Will there be, like, girls?" asks Gaynor.

"Yes," I assure him. "They have girls in other countries, too."

"Awesome. How about tattoo artists?"

"I imagine you will find them wherever we travel," says Pierce, our resident brainiac and walking, talking TripAdvisor. "For instance, the Maori people of New Zealand have long practiced a type of tattooing known as *ta moko*, which is traditionally done with chisels."

Gaynor gulps a little when he hears that.

"I'll, uh, pass on the New Zealand chisel dudes…"

"Yeah," I say. "Me too."

He grins and fist-bumps Pierce. "Then we're in. World, here we come!"

Chapter 21

LEAVING ON A JET PLANE

Poor Uncle Frankie and Aunt Flora.

They barely have time to unpack their honeymoon suitcases. They come home on Wednesday, pass out a few souvenir Niagara Falls snow globes on Friday, repack their bags, and, on Monday, head to Teterboro Airport in New Jersey with me, Gilda, Gaynor, and Pierce.

Stevie's riding to the airport in the Smiley-mobile with the rest of his family. His mom insisted on giving us all a "proper airport good-bye."

"We're so proud of you, Jamie," says Aunt Smiley as she leans in to give me a hug before I board Air Funny One. "Now the whole world will be your stage! That's seven point five billion people for you to make laugh."

"All at the same time," adds Uncle Smiley.

"No, dear," says his wife. "They're all in different time zones."

"Oh. Remember that, Stevie," Uncle Smiley tells his son. "And be sure to set your watch accordingly."

"Will do, Dad." Stevie turns to me. "You want I should sweep the plane? Make sure it's secure?"

"Um, I think those guys already did." I gesture toward the two musclemen in dark suits and sunglasses eyeballing everybody's luggage. Mr. Amodio's goon squad.

"Who are those two?" asks Stevie.

"Your helpers."

"Good. I'll train them later. Right now, I'm getting on board. Want to check out the galley. Taste-test your food. Make sure nobody poisoned anything."

He heads up the steps into the jet. Gilda, Gaynor, and Pierce follow him and keep shouting cool stuff out the door.

"We have two pilots, two copilots, and three flight attendants!" shouts Pierce.

"Everybody gets their own video screen and you can watch movies or play games!" adds Gaynor. "Except the pilots. They don't get screens. They need to, you know, fly the plane."

94

"The galley is full of food!" cries Stevie. "Good stuff. Woo-hoo! We have a popcorn machine and a rolling hot dog griller!"

"Plus chocolate milk," adds Gilda.

Everything the guys are reporting sounds great. But what I love most about Air Funny One is the transfer chair and hydraulic lift attached to the staircase.

I'm flying first class before I'm even inside the jet.

"Everybody strapped in?" asks Uncle Frankie when the flight attendants close the boarding door.

"I'll check," says Stevie, unbuckling his seat belt and walking up the aisle.

"Sir?" says one of the flight attendants. "The pilot can't taxi to the runway until everyone is properly seated."

"Which means he'll never have to wait for me," I crack.

Stevie bustles back to his seat. Straps on his belt. The jet engines whirr and whine as we roll across the tarmac and head for the runway.

"Next stop, Rio," says the pilot over the intercom.

Uncle Frankie starts singing a song none of us have ever heard.

"When my baby, when my baby smiles at me I go to Rio...de Janeiro...My-oh me-oh..."

Fortunately, the jet engines drown him out before he can do the second verse. Aunt Flora is the only one who can hear what he sings next.

It must be kind of funny.

Because she sure is smiling.

Chapter 22

"MY-OH ME-OH, WELCOME TO RIO"

Rio de Janeiro is amazing!

Wow, kiddo! Rio is welcoming you with open arms!

You might remember Rio from the 2016 Olympics. Or that animated movie *Rio* with the macaw from Minnesota and all the other brightly colored birds.

It's the most famous city in Brazil, which is the largest country in South America. It's covered in Amazonian rain forests, and the climate is tropical here. Meaning, I start sweating before the competition even starts.

"Six million people live in Rio," reports Pierce as we wind our way through heavy traffic.

"Did they all have to get in their cars at the same time?" grouses Stevie.

Me? I'm enjoying the scenery, which Gilda, of course, is shooting with her video camera. She's getting some great shots for the next season of *Jamie Funnie!*

We're being chauffeured in an awesome Brazilian limo to the very famous, more-than-one-hundred-year-old Teatro Municipal, which was completely renovated back in 2009. Mr. Amodio's production company is renting the theatrical palace for the Americas finals of the Planet's Funniest Kid Comic competition in Rio.

We check in and check out the stage. It's amazing.

After testing the sound system and visiting my dressing room, we hop back into the limo and go grab something to eat. I gobble down some *brigadeiros* (sweet chocolate balls rolled in chocolate sprinkles) and my new fave, *pao de queijo*—also known as cheesy bread. Stevie goes for the barbecued beef,

99

sausages, and cheese-on-a-stick. Gilda, Gaynor, and Pierce are more adventurous. They order something called *moqueca*, which is pronounced "moo-kek-a" and sounds like a cow with a cough. It's fish stew. It smells like Long Beach after the tide rolls out.

After lunch, the limo takes us on a quick swing past the fabulous Ipanema and Copacabana beaches (we don't have time for a swim), then back to the theater to prep for the taping of the TV show.

Backstage, I see a bunch of nervous comics from Mexico, Brazil, Jamaica, Peru—a dozen kids from all over the Americas.

I also see a bunch of stage moms and dads. They're all pushing their kids a little too hard for my taste (and you know I don't like *anybody* pushing me). We have stage parents in the USA, too. I've seen dozens of them. I sometimes get the feeling that they're putting pressure on their kids to succeed so they can live out their own showbiz dreams—the ones that maybe never came true.

"Oh, look, it's Jamie Grimm!" gushes one of the mothers. "Make him laugh, Hugo. *Ele é um dos juízes*."

"He is one of the judges?" says a confused crew

member with a clipboard who understands Portuguese way better than me. (I thought the stage mom was ordering two juices.) "I thought Jamie Grimm was the master of ceremonies."

"I am," I say.

"We brought you a present from Jamrock, mon," says a stage father with a Jamaican accent. He hands me a canvas bag with Bob Marley's face silkscreened on the sides. Inside, there are jingling bottles of a grapefruity soda called Ting.

"I'm not a judge," I try to explain.

"We'll make you empanadas!" screams a stage mother.

"Churros!" shouts another.

All of a sudden, I'm wishing I could disappear into the real world with Uncle Frankie and Aunt Flora, where I might be able to magically turn into nobody special.

Then the only Peruvian, Brazilian, Jamaican, or Mexican food I'd ever eat would come from Ay Caramba Express back home in Long Beach!

Chapter 23

THEY FUNNY

My job in these regional shows is pretty easy.

I just have to introduce the acts and maybe ad-lib something semifunny. I've always found it sort of easy, as an emcee, to riff off whatever's going on around me. You don't have to write a lot of material. You just have to keep your eyes and ears open and be ready for anything.

The voting in these regional rounds is done by a panel of five judges—all of them local celebrities. When we get to the finals in London, the worldwide TV audience will do the voting via texts, phone calls, and online polls.

The first kid up in Rio is a Jamaican joker named Dequain Dixon. I think his dad was the one who gave me the Ting soda. Dequain does a funny bit about how he can't wait to go on vacation. To Canada. In the winter.

"You know, the beach can be sooooo boring. Every day, mon. Perfect weather. Bright sunshine. Sandy beaches. Crystal-clear water. Me? I want some snow, baby. And gray skies. Canada, that's what I'm talking about, eh? I want to wear mittens and one of those puffy North Face parkas. By the way, what are mittens? Is that what Canadians call baby mice?"

I really like the kid from Mexico, fourteen-year-old Miguel Ángel Gonzalez. He doesn't have a stage mother or father. In fact, he's an orphan who's been doing street comedy for a couple of years, trying to work his way out of the slums of Mexico City.

He does a funny bit in costume and skeleton-face makeup where he pretends he's one of the dear departed souls who's come back from the grave to celebrate *el Día de los Muertos* (the Day of the Dead) with his descendants.

"You know, on *el Día de los Muertos* in Mexico, everybody makes shrines, with photos of their deceased relatives. Then they put on shell necklaces and dance around. You ever dance with seashells jangling around your neck? You make so much noise, you're guaranteed to wake the dead. 'Yo. Family. Knock it off. I was trying to take a dirt nap.'"

The judges vote two comics on to the finals in London: my favorite, Miguel from Mexico, and a sassy girl named Gabriela Guarachi from Peru (her big line: "Send me to London. Alpaca my bags.")

Even though it's after midnight when we wrap, we dash off to the airport. It's a very long flight from Rio to Sydney, Australia—seventeen hours and nineteen minutes if we take the shortcut across Antarctica. I guess that's why we have two teams of pilots and copilots.

Everybody climbs aboard Air Funny One, laughing and talking about what a great time they had at the show and in Rio.

Except for Stevie, Gaynor, and Pierce.

They ate a little too much street food, including mystery meat on a stick. They also drank some water that they probably shouldn't have.

Too bad our jet only has one bathroom, which my three friends keep taking turns visiting. For about seventeen hours and nineteen minutes.

Chapter 24

THE WONDERS DOWN UNDER

When we land in Sydney, everybody is totally fried.

Talk about jet lag. We flew across the International Date Line all the way into tomorrow!

When the pilots open the main cabin door, two uniformed Australian customs officials come on board. They're both clutching spray cans of disinfectant and insecticide.

"G'day, mates," says one as he starts spritzing something that smells like Lysol. "Pardon our quarantine. Because of our isolated location, Australia has been spared many diseases. Want to make certain that no dodgy germs or mozzies hitched a ride with you folks. Ta!"

"Give it a burl, mate," says Uncle Frankie. He and Aunt Flora studied Australian slang on the flight from Rio. "That's a bonzer bloke."

"We haven't seen any mosquitos on board," adds Aunt Flora.

"True," says Gilda. "The only annoying whining on the flight was coming from Stevie."

"The flight *and* the line to the bathroom were so long!" says Stevie as he cranks up his elbow to show his underarm to the customs officer closest to him. "You want to hit my pits?"

"Not necessary, mate," she says. "Good on you for offering."

Then they spray us down. They spray our suitcases, our cell phones, our shoes.

They even spray my wheelchair.

Once we're through customs and on the special shuttle bus Mr. Amodio arranged for us, we swing by the Sydney Harbor Bridge. It's the world's largest steel arch bridge. Then we stop by the Sydney Opera House. It sort of looks like an upside-down turtle convention. Or a bunch of bleached penguin beaks. Or a stack of conquistador helmets. Take your pick.

"Seriously, you guys," says Stevie. "I want to wrestle a crocodile."

"I just want to sleep," I say with a big yawn.

"You can sleep when you're someplace boring, Jamie," says Gilda. "This is Australia!"

That's when two more shuttle vans pull up.

A camera crew tumbles out of the first one, followed by a group of kids with their parents. The second van is carrying even more kids and parents.

"G'day, Jamie," says a young lady. "I'm Olivia. Joe

Amodio sent me. We're going to shoot some B-roll of you meeting our fair dinkum Oz comics."

B-roll is what TV people call the "cutaway" footage that they sprinkle into background or local color stories. Fair dinkum Oz comics? Uncle Frankie translates: "Real-deal Australian comedians."

"These must be the competitors for the Australian region," adds Aunt Flora.

"Koo-wee, you're Jamie Grimm!" gushes an Australian stage mother (yes, they have them in the land down under, too). "I'm tickled pink to meet the funniest kid on the planet!"

"Well, last year's model," says her husband. "Righto, mate?"

"We flew all the way from New Zealand," says another. "Wait until you hear our hardout little Kiwi, Charlotte. Faa! She'll make you laugh louder than a kookaburra!"

I turn to Uncle Frankie.

"It's a bird. Not a crazy donkey."

I shake a bunch of hands. Meet and greet the comics and their families. Stevie and the team of security guards make sure I don't get crushed.

"Hi," says one of the young comics, a cool-looking

kid in sunglasses. He holds out his hand. About six inches away from where it needs to be if he really wants me to shake it. "I'm Hamish Gadsby. So, Jamie, do you know why kangaroos hate rainy days?"

"No, why?"

"Their children want to play inside. Lazy little pouch potatoes…"

I chuckle. Hamish smiles.

"Pleasure to meet you, Mr. Grimm. I've never actually seen your act. But I've heard it."

That's when I finally notice Hamish's white cane. He's blind!

Chapter 25

TWO COMICS, ONE MISSION

I like hanging out with Hamish because, well, I've never met another comedian with what the rest of the world would call a disability.

He's blind, I can't walk. Together, we share a singular, heroic mission: to boldly go where everybody else has gone before. And to crack a few jokes along the way.

We check out my suite at the Four Seasons Hotel.

"Posh place you have here, mate," says Hamish when I roll and he taps his way into the room.

"Um, how do you know it's posh if you can't see it?" I ask.

"Smells posh. Carpet feels extremely cushy, too."

"You want to watch the TV?" asks Hamish. "Or as I call it, 'listen to the radio'?"

"Nah," I say. "Let's just hang and order room service."

"What do you kids want?" asks Uncle Frankie, popping in from his adjoining suite.

"How about some Twisties and Clinkers?"

"What are those?" I ask.

"Delicious Aussie junk food," cracks Hamish.

"Cheese curls and chockies. But stay away from the Vegemite."

"I agree," says Aunt Flora, coming into my side of the suite. "According to the guide book, it's mashed yeast."

"It's also disgusting," says Hamish. "And I'm told it looks worse than it tastes."

We order up a proper Aussie lunch from room service. Uncle Frankie tells the kitchen to "toss a few shrimp on the barbie." Hamish and I order burgers and chips, which are fries. Then Hamish entertains us all with what I'm guessing are some bits from his act.

"I always tell the audience I'm blind right away. Otherwise, they might wonder why I needed somebody to walk me onstage and hand me a microphone. Might look like I don't know where I am or what I'm doing there." He shifts into his preschool teacher voice. "'Okay, welcome to the comedy club, Hamish. Here. You're gonna need this. We call it the microphone. And that out there, that's the audience.' Of course, when you're blind, some of your other senses compensate and become more acute. For instance, my sense of smell." He sniffs the air. "Whoo. Jamie just farted. Either that or somebody opened a jar of Vegemite…"

We're all cracking up.

"You know the worst part about being blind? Going to the movies. Especially the superhero ones with tons of action. When I go see *Thor* or *Wonder Woman*, all I hear is dramatic music and a bunch of explosions. If I wanted to listen to that, I could stay home and slide an iPhone into the toaster."

After lunch, when Uncle Frankie and Aunt Flora go sightseeing, Hamish and I swap stories about what it's like to be us in a world where we don't really fit in.

"I hate when people feel sorry for me," I say.

"Me too," says Hamish. "Or when they say something like 'Oh, from your emails I couldn't tell you were blind.' But don't let it get you down, mate. Keep funny and carry on."

I nod. "When life gives you lemons, learn how to juggle."

"Sorry," says Hamish. "No can do. I have terrible hand-eye coordination."

The more we talk, the more I hope Hamish makes it all the way to the finals in London. He's funny. And he's superreal. Plus, if he *does* compete against me in London, nobody (including Vasily Vasilovich) will be able to say I have an unfair advantage because of my wheelchair.

Hey, Hamish has a white cane.

(I wonder if he knows it's white?)

Chapter 26

AWESOME AUSSIES

We tape the Sydney round of the Planet's Funniest Kid Comic competition at a big TV studio.

There are about five hundred people in the audience.

"G'day, everybody," I say at the top of the show. "You know, yesterday my uncle asked a waiter to have the chef 'toss a few shrimp on the barbie.' He thought he was ordering grilled shrimp. Imagine his surprise when the waiter came back with a blond doll covered with crustaceans."

The crowd laughs. Probably because there's a big sign flashing LAUGH at them.

"I'm your host for the evening, Jamie Grimm."

Now the crowd applauds. Australians are really good at reading blinking signs.

"You guys have some interesting wildlife. If I go to the outback, I think there are at least one hundred and fifty different animals or insects that can kill me. So I bought a boomerang for self-defense. You know what you call a boomerang that won't come back? A stick."

I earn some polite chuckles, feel glad I'm not actually in the competition, and introduce a young comic from New Zealand.

He does a whole set about *The Lord of the Rings*, because those movies were filmed in New Zealand.

"I'm working on writing a sequel, *The Lord of the Onion Rings*. Unless KFC wants to sponsor it. Then I'll change the title to *The Lord of the Wings*."

There must be a GROAN sign, too. Because that's what the audience does.

The next comic is Suzannah Katris from Perth, in Western Australia. She has a very dry, deadpan delivery. Instead of one-liners, she does two-liners. The crowd loves her.

"My boyfriend told me I was drawing my eyebrows too high. I just looked at him, surprised. My mother accused me of being immature. I told her to get out of my crib. Parallel lines have so much in common.

It's a shame they'll never meet. How do you think the unthinkable? With an ithe-berg."

The audience is laughing at Suzannah even before the flashing signs tell them to.

Hamish is the last comic onstage. And yes, some-one does lead him out to the microphone.

"Good evening, ladies and gentlemen, if that's what you are. You could be sheep and goats for all I know. In case the white cane and sunglasses didn't give it away, I'm blind.

118

"I wish I had a guide dog," says Hamish. "Then when I fart, I could blame it on him. Of course, that's why so many blind people don't skydive. It scares the heck out of the dog. The other day, my mother handed me a cheese grater. It was the most violent book I've ever read."

He launches into a funny story.

"A blind rabbit and a blind snake run into each other on the road one day. The snake reaches out, touches the rabbit, and says, 'Oooh, you're soft and fuzzy and have floppy ears. You must be a rabbit.' The rabbit reaches out, touches the snake, and says, 'You're slimy, beady-eyed, have a forked tongue, and slither along the ground. You must be a politician.'"

The crowd roars with laughter.

Three hours later, we have our Australian winners. The girl from Perth comes in second. Hamish takes first.

I'm thrilled for him!

But early in the morning, as I lie awake in my strange hotel bed, staring up at the dark ceiling, I have to wonder: Did Hamish win because of the sympathy vote?

Did people vote for the blind comedian because they felt sorry for him?

It's a possibility, I guess.

One that makes me wonder if I won all my championships the exact same way.

Did people vote for me because of my chair?

It's something I can ponder for the rest of this trip around the world.

Because word comes from New York that Joe Amodio loves, loves, *loves* Hamish Gadsby (and the TV ratings he rings up). In fact, he wants Hamish to fly along with us for the rest of the tour!

I think it'll be awesome to have a second comedian with disabilities on the tour with us. After all, the more of us the world sees, the more common we'll seem!

Chapter 27

LOCAL COLOR

We have a group call on speakerphone with Mr. Amodio at the airport before boarding Air Funny One for the flight up to Tokyo, Japan, for the third regional show.

"Hamish, *bubelah?* Can you hear me?"

"Yes, sir," says Hamish. "So far, my blindness hasn't affected my ears."

"See? That's funny. You hear that, Grimm? He funny."

"Yes, sir," I say. "He definitely is."

"Let me put this on the stoop and see if the cat licks it up," says Mr. Amodio. It's what he always says before he tells us his latest big idea. "In every city we visit, Hamish can be our local color commentator. Gilda?"

"Yes, sir?"

"You have your camera?"

"Always, Mr. Amodio."

"Perfect. Follow Hamish around Tokyo. Have someone, a local, describe the sights to him. Hamish can riff and react and talk about the sounds, the smells. It will be high-larious while simultaneously tugging at everybody's heartstrings. We're talking gold, people. Ratings gold!"

"Um, you want me in those walk-arounds?" I ask. Not that I can actually walk around.

"No, Jamie. We get enough of you during the show. Hamish will give us our feature fillers. The bumpers on either side of the commercial breaks."

Hamish packs his bags in no time. "I wear the same thing every day. I have several sets of the same clothes. It's like a uniform. That way I know everything matches no matter what I put on."

"Will one of your parents be coming with us?" asks Uncle Frankie.

"No," says Hamish very quickly. "I mean, they can't. My father is a famous crocodile wrangler. They need him at the zoo. And my mother? Well, she has a singing gig in Tamworth, the country music capital of 'Stralia."

"Showbiz runs in the family, huh?" says Uncle Frankie with a warm smile.

"Right."

"Well, we'd be happy to be your chaperones," says Aunt Flora.

"Maybe one of your folks could sign a paper or something?" suggests Uncle Frankie.

"Already did, mate." Hamish fumbles for a folded letter in his pocket. "Here you go. The ridgy-didge deal."

Uncle Frankie checks out the letter. Tucks it into his shirt pocket. "Welcome to the family!" he says. "And Jamie Grimm's globe-trotting comedy caravan!"

Stevie actually helps Hamish board the plane.

I think it's great to have Hamish along for the ride. We spend the first hour of the nine-hour flight to Tokyo swapping jokes, trying to one-up each other. It's like a rap battle with punch lines instead of rhymes. The next eight hours? While everybody else naps or fiddles with the movies on their video screens, Hamish and I are just two kids who've faced some pretty tough bumps on the road of life. We talk about what it's like to be have a disability in a way that I haven't talked to almost anybody since I checked out of the rehab hospital.

Hamish gets me. I get him.

And, on Air Funny One, we both get ice cream!

Chapter 28

HELLO, TOKYO

When we land in Japan, we discover that while we've been airborne, Mr. Amodio has been busy working the phones.

We do another speakerphone chat with him while we're parked on the tarmac.

"There's a great Japanese kid in the Tokyo competition named Ichika," says Mr. Amodio. "I have a hunch she'll wind up as one of the top two in the Asian regionals."

"Um, how can you know that?" I ask, hoping that the answer isn't *"because the whole contest is rigged."*

"I feel it in my gut, kid," says Mr. Amodio. "Plus the name Ichika means 'Best Entertainer'! I think, anyway. So how can she lose if she's already the best? Am I right or am I right?"

"Well…"

"I want Ichika to take you guys on a whirlwind tour of Tokyo. Her English is excellent. She can describe stuff to Hamish."

"I thought you didn't want me in those local color segments."

"I changed my mind. Because, Jamie?"

"Yes, sir?" I'm dreading what he might say next.

"I saw Ichika's audition piece. She did a bit about the whole reason she wanted to enter this competition in the first place."

I'm afraid to ask. "And what was that?"

"Ichika wants to meet you, Jamie baby! The girl's crushing on you, big-time. We add a dash of romance to the sympathy stew we got going with you and Hamish and BOOM! Our ratings are going through the roof."

Okay. That bit about the "sympathy stew" makes me think about quitting. Saying *sayonara* to Japan before I even roll off the jet. But then I think about how much fun Hamish is having. How being added to this trip is a huge break for him. Gilda, Gaynor, Pierce, and Stevie are having fun, too. Then there's Uncle Frankie and Aunt Flora enjoying their second honeymoon.

Heavy sigh.

I just need to keep funny and carry on.

Ichika meets us outside the superfamous Sensoji Temple, an ancient Buddhist temple in the Asakusa district of Tokyo. It's the oldest temple in the city. It's also extremely beautiful.

So is Ichika.

Gaynor, who's crewing for Gilda's video shoot with Pierce, falls in love with her immediately. So does Stevie.

When we're done shooting the "local color" piece, Ichika starts giggling.

"I can't believe you're really you!" she says to me.

"I have the same trouble sometimes," I joke.

"You're so funny!" she titters. "And soooooo cute!"

"Is he?" says Hamish. "I haven't felt his face yet..."

"You know," she says, "in Japan we invented Hello Kitty. But I have an even better idea. Hello Jamie!"

"Oh-kay," says Gilda, kind of shepherding Ichika away from me. "Good-bye, Ichika. We'll see you at the show. We've got to move to the next location..."

"We do?" moans Gaynor. "But I haven't even given Ichika my digits..."

"She doesn't want them," says Stevie. "Because I'm going to give her mine."

"No, thank you, boys," says Ichika firmly. Then she wiggle-waggles her hand next to her ear like it's a phone and mouths "Call me"—and winks.

"Jamie?" says Gilda, arching an eyebrow.

"Sorry, Ichika. No time for phone calls. We've got a show to do!"

"And I need to feel Jamie's face," says Hamish. "I just don't see what you girls see in him. Seriously. I don't see it at all."

Chapter 29

FROM RUSSIA WITHOUT LOVE

As Joe Amodio predicted, Ichika will be on the Asian team at the finals in London.

She did a very funny bit about, you guessed it, Hello Jamie. Apparently, I need to paint my wheelchair pink. And wear a pink bow in my hair.

"You also need to erase your mouth," she suggested. "Hello Kitty has no mouth. Just eyes, nose, and whiskers. And a bow." After she was done having fun with me, she riffed on sushi. "It's raw fish," she said. "What people in America call bait."

She also did an epic run on the word *wasabi*—that green, sinus-clearing hot mustard goop they serve with sushi—that ended up with it becoming the Japanese equivalent of "Wassup!"

Second place went to a tall Chinese guy named Zhou Yang. He did a bit about how unfair it was that the contestants had to do their routines in English.

WASABI!

"Why not Chinese? It's the number one language in the world. English? Number three. You blokes are behind Spanish. Besides, English adds so many words. Chinese checkers? How about plain old checkers? Chinese food? Hello? To us, it's just food. And what's up with this expression you have about a bull in a China shop? No matter what you think, in China, we don't encourage barnyard animals to go shopping…"

That night at our hotel, Hamish and I are hanging out when Gilda bursts into my room with her laptop. Stevie is right behind her.

"You guys?" she says. "You have got to see this!"

"Sorry," says Hamish. "No can do."

"Right. My bad."

"I'll describe it to you," says Stevie, pounding his

fist into his palm. "There's this pudgy Russian dude talking trash about Jamie on the internet."

"Is it Vasily Vasilovich?" I ask.

"Yep. I want to punch him."

"Who's Vasily Vasilovich, mate?" asks Hamish.

"A young Russian comic who thinks he's going to win the Planet's Funniest Kid Comic Contest," I explain. "He's been taunting me online for a few weeks now."

"On the internet?" asks Hamish.

"Yeah."

"You know one of the few advantages of being blind? You never have to look at pop-up ads."

"You guys?" says Gilda, sounding frustrated. "Vasily is getting serious."

"Really?" says Hamish. "Did he forget that this is a comedy competition?"

"Just listen."

Gilda clicks a key and another video scrolls across her screen.

"Greetings, Jamie Greem. I have seen your shows from Brazil and Australia. What is the matter? Why do you not even attempt to be funny? Your jokes are old and tired. Maybe this is why you need the wheelchair. You are actually a little old man. With a bad haircut."

"You better watch out for this Hamish from Australia, Jamie Greem," Vasily continues. "He is not funny, either, but he might steal away many of your seeempathy votes. See you both in London. Because I am not blind. Get it? I make Hamish joke. You are now permitted to laugh."

The video fades to black.

So does my mood.

Hamish's, too.

"Catch you guys in the morning," he mumbles.

"See you then," I mumble back.

Hamish is so bummed, he doesn't even snap back with "Wish I could say the same" like he usually does.

Chapter 30

KENYA BELIEVE IT? WE'RE IN AFRICA

When we land in Nairobi, Kenya, guess who gets the big hero's welcome?

Not me. My buddy Jimmy Pierce! Apparently, they watch *Jamie Funnie* all over Africa and Pierce is everybody's favorite character. Maybe because he's African-American. Maybe because (in life and on the show) he's supersmart and extremely nice. Either way, hundreds of his fans have come out to greet him—all of them dressed in his signature porkpie hat. A bunch are sporting his thick-rimmed smart-guy glasses, too.

Hamish does some sightseeing with Gilda and

her camera. A funny girl named Chiku (which, by the way, is Swahili for "chatterer") is their tour guide. She's also a contestant in the competition. Gilda shows me the footage backstage at the Kenya National Theatre, where we'll be taping the African regionals.

Hamish and Chiku visited the Giraffe Centre, about three miles from the middle of Nairobi.

"I think you'll really, really, really like it here, but I'm not going to tell you exactly where we are because that would, like, totally ruin the surprise." Chiku lives up to her name. She is very chatty. "Hey, Hamish?"

"Yes, Chiku?"

"What did the leopard say after eating its trainer?"

"Man, that hits the spot."

"Oh. You've heard that one."

"Yes. Back when I was in kindergarten."

The video shifts to Hamish and Chiku standing outside a pen where a ginormous giraffe is nibbling leaves off a twenty-foot-tall tree.

"What smells like horse manure?" asks Hamish.

"A tall creature with long legs and an extremely long neck," says Chiku. "She kind of reminds me of a supermodel. But this creature's fur coat is spotted with brown splotches like camouflage, which is why I almost didn't see her…"

"Well, at least you finally did," cracks Hamish. "I've got nothing."

"She also has two bumps or horns on top of her head."

"Crikey. It sounds like a mutant unicorn!"

"Would you like to pet her?" asks Chiku.

"No, thanks, mate. I'm blind, not crazy."

It's pretty funny.

So are the comedians who take the stage that night at the theater. In fact, in my humble opinion, the African comics are far and away the funniest we've seen so far on the tour.

Seems that some African comics like to make fun of other countries' football (meaning soccer) teams. So the guy from Botswana makes fun of the soccer team from South Africa, while the South African comic makes fun of the team from Zimbabwe. The funniest part about the bits? They all use, basically, the same jokes.

Chapter 31

CHEERS FOR CHIKU

I roll onstage after the South African comic, Demarco Coetzee (who does a very good impersonation of Trevor Noah from *The Daily Show*), does his final Zimbabwe soccer joke.

"Let's hear it for Demarco," I say. "You know, hearing all these soccer jokes, it reminds me of things I'll never be able to do. Like play soccer. Not because I can't kick the ball. Because I don't understand the rules. What's a striker? A guy who doesn't want to play so he walks around the field chanting and carrying a picket sign? Some other things I'll never do? Sneak up on you on tiptoe. Break-dance. Skydive. Well, I guess I *could* skydive. But if I did, I'd probably total my chair."

I enjoy my laughs and introduce Chiku.

She bounds onstage and launches into a rapid-fire set that cracks everybody up.

"Hello, everybody. *Sasa?* How you doing? I am Chiku Jemaiyo and I am from Kenya, so right off the top let's get one thing straight—I do not run marathons. Twenty-six miles? *Haiya!* Are you kidding? I'm only running twenty-six miles if an elephant is chasing me the whole way. And he better poke me in the butt with his tusks to keep me motivated.

There's an old Kenyan proverb: "He who runs alone celebrates." I guess because he is just competing against himself. Or because nobody's looking, so he can just walk or call a taxi.

"Speaking of being chased by wild beasts, the other day my teacher asked me, 'Chiku, if a lion is chasing you, what will you do?' 'Climb a tree, teacher,' I told him. 'What if the lion climbs a tree?' 'Then I will jump in the river and swim.' 'But what if the lion also jumps into the river and swims after you?' 'Whoa, brudda,' I told him. 'Whose side are you on? Mine or the lion's?'"

The crowd roars.

Chiku and Demarco take first and second place. They'll be joining us in London for the finals.

After the show, we have a huge celebration. There's music, food, dancing, and, of course, more jokes. Gilda and I get hoisted in the air in our chairs because, apparently, the video of our goofy dance at Uncle Frankie's wedding has gone viral.

By the way, Kenyan barbecue pizza is awesome. They bake it in a charcoal oven called a *jiko* and top it with stuff like cheese, chorizo, chilies, and corn. Delish!

"This is so great," I say, wolfing down my third slice. "I never want to leave Nairobi."

"Me neither," says Uncle Frankie. "And not because of the pizza."

He and Aunt Flora look superworried.

"What's up?" I ask.

"We're just a little nervous, hon," says Aunt Flora. "About the next stop on the tour."

"Dubai?" I say. "Why?"

"We just heard from Mr. Amodio," says Uncle Frankie. "He told us to 'expect fireworks.'"

"I like fireworks," says Gilda. "Especially on the Fourth of July."

Uncle Frankie shakes his head. "I don't think Mr. Amodio was talking about the whiz-bang sparkly kind, kiddo. I think he means there could be trouble."

Chapter 32

ISRAELI-PALESTINIAN CONFLICT

Unless you've been living under a rock for most of your life, you know there are all sorts of political tensions in the Middle East.

It's been like that for decades, maybe centuries.

And probably will be for decades, maybe centuries, more.

Sometimes those tensions bubble up into actual shooting wars. I'm thinking that's why Uncle Frankie and Aunt Flora are so nervous about the next stop on our world comedy tour.

"It's worse," Frankie tells me on the flight from Nairobi to Dubai. "Joe Amodio wants to exploit that bad blood for what he calls 'boffo numbers.' He thinks pitting an Israeli comic against a Palestinian will really boost our ratings."

Another news flash for any under-a-rock dwellers: The Israelis and Palestinians don't always get along. They're like oil and water. Toothpaste and orange juice. Peanut butter and tuna.

An Israeli comic going up against a Palestinian? There really could be some fireworks. And like Uncle Frankie said—they won't be the pretty kind with marching band music, either.

"We should check these two jokers out," suggests Hamish. "There has to be video on them."

"There is," says Uncle Frankie. "Mr. Amodio uploaded a file. It's on your video screen, Jamie."

I turn to Hamish and Gilda. "Should we watch it?"

"You guys go ahead," says Hamish. "I'll just eavesdrop."

I tap and swipe my video screen. The first young comedian is a guy named Benji Yatzpan from Tel Aviv, Israel.

After a few classic old-school one-liners about his girlfriend, his mom, and gefilte fish, Benji launches into a story joke.

"An old man is on his deathbed. His daughter is dutifully there. And he says, very weakly, 'I smell kugel.' The daughter says, 'Yes, Father. Mother is making noodle kugel.' The old man is just about to pass away. He's on his last breaths. He says to his daughter, 'Oh, to taste noodle kugel once more before I die.' And she says, 'Of course, Father.'

144

"So she runs into the kitchen, comes back, sits down. She folds her hands over her empty lap. The old man speaks—barely even able to utter the words—'Where's the kugel?' And his daughter tells him, 'Mom says it's for after.'"

The guy's great. His material is mostly self-deprecating, which means he's making fun of himself and his culture, not any lifelong enemies.

Next we watch Fadi Hanania, the Palestinian comic.

"My mom never really says she loves me. She just cooks me my favorite food. Because, in my house, food equals love. If we had Valentine's Day, we'd give each other falafel."

Hearing Fadi's routine about his mom, I grin.

I think I might know how to achieve peace in the Middle East!

Chapter 33

THE DUEL IN DUBAI?

When we land in Dubai—which, by the way, has the most incredible skyline of any city I've ever seen—Joe Amodio is waiting for us at the airport.

And yes, the airport is awesome, too. It's like a shopping mall where the parking lot is full of jets instead of Volkswagen Jettas.

We load our bags (and me) into another shuttle bus and drive into the city.

"Quick," says Hamish. "Somebody describe the skyline to me. When we were making our final approach into the airport, Jamie said it was amazing."

"It is," says Stevie. "Very shiny and pointy. Except one skyscraper that was kind of twisty."

"It's even more amazing at night," says Mr. Amodio. "So many colored lights."

"I'll take your word for it," says Hamish.

"Good," says Mr. Amodio. "Because we're gonna skip the local-color-tour bit on this stop."

"How come?" I ask.

"Because we've got much better material. Benji versus Fadi. Israeli against Palestinian. Why do you think I personally flew in for this round? We're gonna put them in the same dressing room, watch the sparks fly."

"Is that wise, Joseph?" asks Uncle Frankie. He only uses somebody's whole first name when he's slightly ticked off at them.

"Wise?" says Mr. Amodio. "No. It's brilliant. Let me tell you a little something about TV, Frankie, baby. Conflict is king. People watch talent shows

148

because conflict is baked into the concept. It's every comic for him- or herself on that stage. And at the end of the day, at the finals in London, there can only be one comedian left standing."

"Or sitting," I toss in. "If, you know, we're being technical…"

"But do you really want to fan the flames of an *international* conflict?" asks Aunt Flora.

"You betcha," says Mr. Amodio. "The bigger the conflict, the better. Hey, like I said before, comedy is a violent sport. Why do you think they call it slapstick? Comedians always say they want to slay the audience. Have them rolling in the aisles. When the crowd roars, comedians say they killed big."

"Some of us just want to hear a few laughs, mate," says Hamish.

"Or make people smile," I add.

Mr. Amodio cringes. "Boys? Please. Don't go all mushy on me. This is my show and you two have to do what I tell you to do. You signed contracts saying I have complete creative control."

"Did I?" said Hamish. "I thought it was a napkin. Of course, I can't really tell the difference…"

"It was a contract," says Uncle Frankie with

149

another heavy sigh. As Hamish's guardian on this trip, he checked over the legal document before he let Hamish sign it.

"Did I use invisible ink?" asks Hamish.

Uncle Frankie shakes his head. "It was blue."

Hamish nods. "Smelled blue."

The shuttle van pulls into the parking lot of the boat-shaped, supermodern Dubai Opera, where we'll be taping the Middle East regionals. The brand-new performing arts center has towering glass walls and sits right next door to the Burj Khalifa, the world's tallest building.

"So, Jamie?" says Mr. Amodio.

"Yes, sir?"

"When you get inside, I want you to immediately roll into their dressing room. Try to stir things up between Benji and Fadi. Maybe get them insulting each other. Some kind of comic put-downs. We have hidden cameras set up behind the mirrors. We'll capture the whole schtick!"

"Okay," I say, with a wink to Uncle Frankie. "No problem. Happy to oblige, sir."

Have I, all of a sudden, gone over to the dark side?

Nope. Don't forget: I have a plan.

Chapter 34

HAPPY MOTHER'S DAY

A techie hooks me up with a wireless microphone backstage.

Joe Amodio scurries off to the control room to watch the dressing room shenanigans on a bank of video monitors. Everybody else traipses along after him except Hamish.

He hangs back and taps me with his cane.

"Did I hit you in the head, mate?" he asks.

"No. That's my shoulder."

"Too bad. I was aiming for your skull, hoping to knock a little sense into your numb noggin. Don't let that daggy doofus Joe Amodio make you do something you're gonna regret, Jamie Grimm. Comedy should bring people together, not tear them apart."

"I completely agree."

"Is that so? Then why are you rolling into that dressing room to muck around with those two blokes?"

"Who says I'm gonna muck around with *them?*"

Hamish thinks about it for a second.

"Oh. Good on you, mate." He starts tapping his way up the hall to join the others in the control room. "This I've got to hear."

I knock on the dressing room door. Somebody grunts, "Come in," so I do.

Benji is sitting at one mirror. Fadi is sitting at another one at the far end of the makeup table. I can't see the cameras hidden behind the mirrors. Neither can they.

"Hi, guys," I say. "I'm Jamie Grimm. And I'm a big fan of your work."

They both nod, well, grimly at me. I get the feeling they don't enjoy being roommates. Especially since their dressing room is so tiny.

"So," I say, "did either of you hear about the guy whose mom texted him to ask 'What do IDK, LY, and TTYL mean?' The guy said, 'I don't know, love you, talk to you later.' 'Okay,' said his mother. 'I'll ask your sister.'"

Benji and Fadi both laugh. One right after the other.

"Speaking of mothers," says Benji. "My mother walked me to the bus stop on my first day of kindergarten. 'Behave, my *bubaleh*,' she said. 'Take good care of yourself and think about your mother, *tataleh!* Then come right back home on the bus, *schein kindaleh*. Your mommy loves you, my *ketsaleh!*' At the end of the day, the bus dropped me off. My mother ran up to me and hugged me. 'So, what did my *pupaleh* learn on his first day of school?' she asked. I told her, 'I learned my name is Benji.'"

I laugh. So does Fadi. Then he launches into a joke of his own: "My mother used to yell at me from the window. 'Come home, Fadi!' 'Why?' I'd ask. 'Am I hungry?' 'No,' she'd say. 'You're cold.'"

"I know a Jewish man who called his mother in Florida," says Benji. "He asked her how she was doing. She said she felt very weak. 'I haven't eaten in thirty-eight days.'"

"I heard the same thing about an Arab man," says Fadi. "He said to his mother, 'That's terrible. Why haven't you eaten in thirty-eight days?'"

Benji picks it back up: "'Because,' answered the

mother, 'I didn't want my mouth to be full of food should you call.'"

When Benji lands the punch line, Fadi slaps him a high five.

Then we all launch into our favorite doting mother jokes.

We're all laughing our heads off, but I think my smile is the biggest.

Mr. Amodio didn't get what he was looking for from these two young comics.

But I sure did.

MO' TENSIONS IN THE MIDDLE EAST

"**T**hat Kumbaya moment with Benji and Fadi was sweet, Jamie baby," says Mr. Amodio when he comes into my dressing room.

"Thanks!" I tell him.

"I was being sarcastic."

Oh.

"I'm sorry, sir, but I just don't think—"

"Like a TV executive!" he finishes for me. "From now on, leave the thinking to me. My job is to blow this show's ratings through the roof so BNC can charge more for the commercials so it can afford to pay for all the jet fuel Air Funny One is guzzling to keep you and your merry entourage flying around the globe!"

I don't think Mr. Amodio has ever been this mad at me. Fortunately, Uncle Frankie hustles into the dressing room.

"What's all the shouting about back here, Joe?" he asks, puffing up his chest like a tough New Yawk pigeon ready to peck somebody in the nose.

"Nothing," says Mr. Amodio. "I was just expressing my disappointment with Jamie's preshow performance."

"Well," says Uncle Frankie, "next time, try to express it a little more politely. *Capisce?* I don't like hearing anybody yelling at my soon-to-be-son. Now, if you don't mind, they need Jamie onstage. He has a comedy show to emcee."

"No problem, Frankie," says Mr. Amodio. "Go out there and kill 'em, kid."

"Again with the violence?" says Uncle Frankie.

Mr. Amodio shrugs. "Like I keep telling you two—comedy is a tough sport. It's like baseball with nothing but bats."

"How does that work?" I say. "Do the players go out there and bonk each other with wooden clubs?"

I do my best to forget that I even know Joe Amodio and focus on giving all the kids stepping into the spotlight of the Middle East regional competition fantastic introductions.

The more of these shows I host, the more I realize that most of the material comes from the same place, no matter where the comic lives. The kid comedians in Dubai make fun of everyday topics like boyfriends and girlfriends, wanting to drive, their moms, cell phones, school, families, how horrible traffic is (even though they can't drive), pop music, football (soccer), hummus, and Facebook. It's the same stuff the comics in Rio, Sydney, Tokyo, and Nairobi were joking about. Except for the hummus.

The judges in Dubai include American comedian Mohammed "Mo" Amer, who fled from Kuwait as a baby during the Gulf War. He did his own set in between kid comedians.

"You know my first name, Mohammed, is the most popular name in the world, okay? You know what's frustrating about that fact? I went to Disney World three weeks ago, not one key chain with my name on it…not a single one."

At the end of the show, Mo Amer and the other judges on the panel make their final cuts. As I hoped, the pair of comedians moving on to the final round in London are Benji Yatzpan and Fadi Hanania.

Their mothers must be so proud!

BYE, BYE, DUBAI

Joe Amodio is almost too excited about Benji and Fadi moving on to the finals.

"This could make up for what happened here," he says the next morning as we're checking out of the hotel, loading up for the trip to the airport and our flight on Air Funny One to Berlin, the capital of Germany. "With those two in the live finals, we'll have another chance for fireworks!"

"I don't like fireworks," says Hamish. "It's just a bunch of pops and crackles way off in the distance. I could have more fun listening to a bowl of Rice Krispies."

"Well, Hamish," Mr. Amodio snaps back, "we'll just have to wait to see what happens."

"Yes," says Hamish. "But according to my doctors,

I will have to wait a long, long, *long* time."

"You're funny, kid," says Mr. Amodio. "You've got me grinning from ear to ear, here."

"Really? I couldn't tell. You're standing in my blind spot. But then again, so is everybody else…"

We all laugh. Except Mr. Amodio. He's in a pretty sour mood. The Middle East regionals didn't work out the way he wanted them to.

"See you folks in Berlin," he says, climbing into his limo. "And I know, Hamish—you wish you could say the same. But I promise you all: we won't have to wait long for those fireworks. The sparks will definitely fly at the European regionals. Bad boy Vasily Vasilovich will be there. They don't call him the Dzerzhinsk Destroyer for nothing!"

Mr. Amodio won't be flying to Berlin with us. He has his own private jet waiting for him at the Dubai airport.

We load into Air Funny One.

"How you feeling?" Gilda asks me when we're all strapped in and taxiing out to the runway.

"Great," I say. "All the comedians so far have been fantastic and funny. I think it's neat how comedy can bring people together."

"Yeah," says Gilda, smiling at me. "I like that, too."

All of a sudden, I have a flashback. To when I first met Gilda Gold. The girl with the frizzy hair I knew from math class.

Pierce introduced us in the cafeteria.

"Gilda's in my robotics club," said Pierce. "She told me she likes those jokes you crack all the time from the back of the room. So I invited her to join us for lunch so she could officially meet you."

I started nodding, staring, and stammering something like "St-st-stammer, stammer, stammer, stammer."

It made Gilda giggle.

"I bet you say that to all the girls," she said, giving me her bubbly laugh.

Which gave *me* enough confidence to say, "No. Usually I say something like 'Haven't I seen you someplace before?' And then the girl says, 'Yeah, that's why I don't go there anymore.'"

Gilda laughed and flung me her own joke: "Yesterday this total jerk actually asked me what my sign was. I told him, 'No Parking.'"

Suddenly, it was like we had this whole history between us, even though we didn't. Just math class.

And a love of jokes, I guess.

So, yeah, it *is* pretty great when comedy can bring people together.

Especially when it brings you together with someone you really like!

Chapter 37

BERLIN FUNNY BUSINESS

We tape our show at the Schiller Theater in Berlin, the venue where they also shot the 2007 season of *Das Supertalent*, the German version of the international *Insert-Country-Name's Got Talent* TV franchise.

It's kind of funny that we're hosting a comedy competition in Germany because, well, the Germans have a reputation for being very precise, rigid, and regimented. Good for making cuckoo clocks. Not so much for comedy.

But the comic representing Germany in the competition, Fritz Fuhrmann, does a great job of spinning that stereotype into comic gold.

"People think we Germans are so uptight and analytical and structured," he says, very sternly. "But that's not true and I'm here to prove it." He pauses and raises a finger. "JOKE NUMBER ONE…"

He also jokes about the Berlin Wall, which used to separate East Berlin from West Berlin back during the Cold War. "My father really misses it. He says ever since they tore it down, his handball game stinks. Of course, we all know why the Berlin Wall fell. It wanted to go down in history."

Amelie Zwiefelhofer, a Swiss comic, does a funny bit about flying over the mountains lining the border between Switzerland and Italy. She puts on a Swiss pilot voice and says, "Uh, if the passengers on the left-hand side of the plane will look out their windows, you will see the Alps. And if the passengers on the right-hand side of the plane will also look left, you will see a bunch of people looking out their windows."

The British, Italian, and Slovenian comics are terrific, too.

But I really, *really* like the French comedian, Jean-Claude Bernard. I guess I like anybody with three first names. But what I love about his act is that it reminds of me of Charlie Chaplin's universal language of silent comedy. Jean-Claude takes the stage and doesn't say a word. Instead, he does this incredible pantomime—the good kind like the clowns in a Cirque du Soleil show might do; not the stuff you see guys in whiteface makeup, berets, and striped shirts do where they pretend they're walking against the wind or trapped inside an invisible box.

It's hysterical.

He's walking his dog when he sees a pretty girl, whom *we* can only see because he pretends he sees her. Judging by the tugs and grunts and grimaces, his dog sees a pretty dog...on the opposite side of the stage from where Jean-Claude has placed his invisible beauty. The tortured tangling of his make-believe leash and his real legs as he tries to flirt with the girl while trying to control the dog, who stops to take a leak on Jean-Claude's leg, brings down the house.

While I'm sitting in the wings, totally enjoying Jean-Claude's silent antics, Stevie, my "bodyguard," comes over.

"I just met Vasily Vasilovich, the Russian dude," he says.

"And?"

Stevie smiles proudly.

"He reminds me of the old me."

Uh-oh.

This can't be good.

Chapter 38

EXTREMELY COLD WAR

As the master of ceremonies, it's my job to introduce Vasily.

My flop sweat has flop sweat. I haven't met the Dzerzhinsk Destroyer in person yet. He's been holed up in his dressing room since he arrived at the theater.

I'm so nervous, I give Vasily the lamest introduction I think I've ever given. "Ladies and gentlemen, there's no time for 'Stalin,' so I'm 'Russian' to bring out our next comic, wh—"

One of the judges bops his buzzer. They only use those when they think an act totally stinks. So far, I'm the first one to get a SKRONK.

"Oh-kay," I say. "W-w-w-without further ado, here he is, straight from Russia, your friend and mine—well, to be honest, I've never actually met the guy, so he's not really my friend—"

SKRONK!

A second judge gives me a buzzer.

I cut to the chase.

"Vasily Vasilovich!"

I roll offstage as quickly as I can with sweat-soaked palms. My hands keep slipping on the rubber as Vasily struts onto the stage, making a grand entrance to the Red Army Men's Chorus singing something so heroically sad it could be from the soundtrack to a Russian submarine movie.

"Good evening, my friends," he says, grabbing the microphone. "Thank you for that wonderful introduction, Jamie Greem. Wait. Check that. I meant to say, 'Thank you for that terrible, horrible, no-good, stinky introduction.' Can you believe this guy? Jamie Greem is supposed to be the funniest kid comic on the planet? Which planet are we talking about here? Pluto? Someplace uninhabited? If you laugh in the vast vacuum of space, does anybody hear you? Jamie Greem will never know. Even if he goes into space, no one will laugh at his jokes. I know, I know. Jamie's fans are all saying, 'You will never find anyone like him.' Precisely. That's the point. Who would want to?"

The audience is chuckling. Me? I'm sort of hiding in the shadows offstage.

Before the show, Jamie Greem tells me he has the body of a Greek god. I have to explain to him that Buddha was not Greek.

"But enough about the unfunniest kid comic on the planet," Vasily continues. "What about the French fraud, Jean-Claude? He has no jokes. He has no dog. He has no voice. I guess his parents told him children are to be seen, not heard. You know what you would get if you ran a mime over with a steamroller? A silent film."

The audience gasps.

Vasily glares at them.

"I kid. Why so serious, peoples? You are now permitted to laugh. And how about our Swiss miss? She is so ugly, when her parents drop her off at school they get a fine for littering."

And on and on it goes. Vasily is vicious. He even makes fun of the judges.

"How many times do I have to flush before you people go away? I kid. You are now permitted to laugh."

Nobody really does.

At the end of the show, Jean-Claude, the silent comedian, is named the top comic in the European round.

But somehow, as mean and awful as he was, Vasily takes second place.

"That was my idea," Joe Amodio brags after the show. "You could say I swayed the judges. After all, I sign their paychecks. And when Vasily takes the stage at the finals in London, the whole world will be tuning in to hear what mean and nasty stuff he'll say next!"

Chapter 39

MY MIDAIR PITY PARTY

"**D**on't let that dude get under your dome," advises Gaynor on the flight from Berlin to London.

"He is, quite simply, a bully," adds Pierce.

"Yeah," says Stevie, with more than a hint of admiration, "I thought *I* was good at talking trash. But that Vasily is one of the best I've ever seen. You gotta admire the guy's work ethic. His craftsmanship…"

"Not me, mate," says Hamish. "I just think he's a big blowhard. Smells like one, too."

"Seriously?" says Gilda. "What's a blowhard smell like?"

"Fish," says Hamish, without missing a beat. "Like the stench that comes out of a beluga whale's blowhole right after a big seafood dinner."

Everybody cracks up. Except Stevie. He taps his

armrest computer screen and starts googling *Vasily Vasilovich*. He even finds a photo of Vasily riding horses with President Vladimir Putin. Neither one has their shirt on.

As much as everybody is trying to get me to laugh off Vasily's insults, it's hard to do. Because a little voice, deep inside my head, way down where they make the earwax, is telling me the mean Russian kid is right. I not funny. I've just rolled into stardom because people feel sorry for me an account of my backstory and wheelchair.

Hamish taps my leg with his cane. "Are you feeling sorry for yourself because you think people have been feeling sorry for you?"

I'm startled. Is my new friend a mind reader? "How'd you know?"

"I could smell the pity party you're throwing yourself over there. I should've baked you a cake."

"So what, exactly, does *pity* smell like?"

"Worse than fish farts, mate. But don't forget, Jamie, in the finals Vasily will be picking on me and Ichika and Chiku and Benji and everybody. You will not be alone. Save some of that pity for the rest of us!"

I grin. "Will do."

I look to the front of the cabin and see Uncle Frankie on the satellite phone. Aunt Flora is with him. He's tugging his hair. She's looking worried.

"Whoa. Slow down, Vinnie. Call my meat guy and tell him you need more hamburger. No, you can't just go to McDonald's and borrow a box of Quarter Pounder patties. Our burgers are eight ounces...not four. Yes, Vinnie, I know four plus four equals eight..."

Aunt Flora sees me listening in to the conversation.

"Trouble at the diner," she tells me. "Vinnie's in a little over his head." She crinkles up her face like she needs to say something that she really doesn't want to say. "We may need to go home. Maybe the Kosgrovs could fly to London and take over the chaperoning duties."

"Whatever you guys need to do," I say.

She grins. Weakly. "Thanks, hon. We'll talk about it more when we land."

Joe Amodio is waiting for us at London's Gatwick Airport. His private jet landed before ours. He's with two very stern-looking characters in stuffy costumes, like on that TV show *Downton Abbey* that Aunt Smiley loved to watch.

"Jamie? Hamish?" says Mr. Amodio. "Meet Reginald and Clarissa. They're your very proper British butler and nanny."

"They smell like starch and raspberry jam," mutters Hamish.

"Um, why do we need a butler and nanny?" I ask.

"Because," says Mr. Amodio, flapping a hand at Uncle Frankie, Aunt Flora, Gilda, Gaynor, Pierce, and Stevie, "it's time for your entourage to go home."

Chapter 40

LONDON BRIDGE IS FALLING DOWN

"**Y**ou're going to be a contestant again, Jamie baby," Mr. Amodio continues. "You're going back into the lions' den. You'll be competing against all the kids who made it to the finals, plus the team from Great Britain."

"There's a team from Great Britain?"

"Yeah," says Joe Amodio. "They're hysterical. We didn't bring them to Berlin because I knew we'd be coming back here and airplane tickets aren't cheap. Neither are private jets. To level the playing field, your crew has to head home. We can't let you have all these flunkies."

"They're not flunkies," I say. "They're my friends and family."

"Even worse," says Mr. Amodio. "You're a star of a BNC sitcom. You're the reigning champion. If we let you keep your own chaperones, your pals, and your personal bodyguard, it'd look like the network was showing favoritism. It'd be a public relations nightmare. For the network, and for you, kiddo."

"Who'll look after Jamie? And Hamish?" asks Uncle Frankie.

"Who'll make sure they eat right and go to bed on time?" asks Aunt Flora.

"That would be me," says Nanny Clarissa.

"Assisted by me," adds the butler. He also clicks his heels.

"It's only for, what, another week or so?" says Mr. Amodio. "You can call Jamie every day. Do video chats. Text. Email."

"Nobody emails anymore, dude," says Gaynor. "It's so, like, 2015."

"I'll be fine," I tell my friends and family. Mostly because I sense that Uncle Frankie needs to rush home to Good Eats by the Sea before his weekend guy, Vinnie, does something really ridiculous—like make egg salad out of hot dogs. Or, even worse, hot dogs out of eggs!

"You sure, Jamie?" asks Uncle Frankie.

I nod.

"I'll look after him," says Hamish. "Not that I'm all that good at literally *looking* at things, but you know what I mean, mate."

Aunt Flora smiles.

It's settled.

Air Funny One will shuttle everybody else back to New York. Hamish and I will check into our London hotel with our nanny and butler.

"When are the live shows?" asks Stevie eagerly.

"This weekend on BNC," says Mr. Amodio. "Eight PM Eastern, seven PM Central. You'll be home in plenty of time to catch the first show—the elimination round."

"Woo-hoo!" says Stevie. "I can't wait to see that Vasily guy in action again. I might start his American fan club!" He glares at me. "You now have permission to laugh, Jamie Greem! See? I've already memorized his catchphrase."

We hug and say our good-byes. Well, Stevie doesn't hug. He's back to giving me head noogies.

He knuckle-rubs my scalp something fierce.

"Just imitating my new hero, cuz!" he shouts. "Vasily is the Russian me!"

Chapter 41

WARM WORDS

Mr. Amodio starts yammering into his phone and walks off to find his limo.

Uncle Frankie says good-bye one last time and leads the way out to the tarmac and Air Funny One. Its engines are already whining.

My stomach ties itself into knots as I watch my family and friends climb aboard.

Before she leaves, however, Gilda comes up to me and whispers a bunch of stuff in my ear.

She has very humid breath. Extremely steamy.

"Don't let them get to you, Jamie. Be who you are," she whispers, "not who they want you to be."

I nod and hope Gilda has more to say. I like her warm words in my ear.

"Joe Amodio is trying to knock you off balance," she continues. "He loves conflict. Makes us bake it into every single episode of *Jamie Funnie*. The best TV for him would be for you to lose your cool and win by going negative, just like Vasily did with you in Berlin. Don't give him what he wants."

"I have cool?" I ask.

"Tons of it," Gilda whispers.

Then she kisses me.

"I heard that!" says Hamish.

"Everything?" asks Gilda.

"No. Just the smacky pash."

"Does that mean kiss?"

"Good on you, Gilda. I also heard what Jamie said about being cool. You're a very good whisperer, Gilda."

"Thanks. Have fun, you guys."

"Right," I say. "Because you can't spell *funny* without *fun!*"

Gilda rolls her eyes, laughs, and hurries out to the jet.

Hamish and I move to the windows and watch Air Funny One as it zooms down the runway and takes off. Well, I watch. Hamish listens. And smells fumes.

"Are you ready, Masters Grimm and Gadsby?" asks the butler when the jet has climbed into the sky. "Your ground transportation awaits."

"I've packed scones, clotted cream, and jam for the ride!" gushes the nanny.

"I told you," Hamish whispers to me. "Raspberry jam."

We crawl through London traffic and make our way to Elstree Studios, where they do *Britain's Got*

Talent and another competition show called *Strictly Come Dancing*. That's one I *won't* be auditioning for.

Mr. Wetmore, the tech director from *Jamie Funnie*, who's great at doing live TV (he used to work on *Saturday Night Live*), will be working these "Comedy Olympics" for BNC because the final shows will be broadcast live. That means we'll have to be funny at 1 AM London time because that's 8 PM New York time!

"Hey, Mr. Wetmore!" I say as I roll and Hamish taps onto the stage. "This is my new friend, Hamish Gadsby."

"Pleased to meet you, Hamish," says Mr. Wetmore. "I've enjoyed watching your antics as you boys trotted around the globe."

"Thank you, sir," says Hamish, shaking Mr. Wetmore's hand, once he finds it. "Jamie's told me all about you. Says if you're on the job, she'll be right."

Mr. Wetmore looks confused. People often do when Hamish whips out his Australian slang.

"*She'll be right* means 'everything will turn out okay,'" I explain.

"Oh. I sure hope so. So, have you two met Milton Cromwell?"

"Nope," I say. "Is he one of the British comedians?"

Mr. Wetmore shakes his head. "He's heading up the judge panel for the finals. And a word of warning, Jamie…"

"Yeah?"

"They don't call him Milton the Meanie for nothing."

Chapter 42

AMAZING GRACE

"So, Jamie, do you know why they call England the wettest country?"

Before I can answer, Grace Garner jumps in with the punch line.

"Because the queen has reigned here for years!"

Friday night, I'm waiting in a holding room backstage with my American teammate, the Corn Queen from Iowa, Grace Garner. She keeps cracking quick jokes like a movie theater popcorn popper that's lost its lid.

"Back home in Iowa, I know a rancher," says Grace. "When he was in his field with his cows, he counted one hundred and ninety-six. But when he rounded them up, he had two hundred."

I smile.

"That's funny," I say.

"Guess that's why you didn't laugh."

"Sorry," I tell her. "I'm just a little nervous."

"Understandable. I'd be nervous if I were you, too. You're the defending world champion. King of the mountain. And tonight, fifteen fierce and funny kid comics want to knock you off your pedestal—including me, of course. Because, let's face it, even though we're 'teammates'…"

She does air quotes.

I'm not crazy about air quotes.

"...we both know there can only be one funniest kid comic on this or any other planet."

"Right," I say, because I know that funni*est* means funnier than every other funny person.

I think about all the great comedians I've seen on my trip around the world. Miguel from Mexico; Gabriela from Peru; Hamish (of course) and Suzannah from Australia; Ichika (the Hello Jamie girl) from Japan; Zhou Yang, the Chinese comic; Chiku from Kenya; Demarco from South Africa; Benji from Israel; Fadi, the Palestinian; Jean-Claude, the French mime; Grace from the USA.

And, of course, from Russia, without love, Vasily Vasilovich.

I also can't forget the two new wild cards. The pair of comics nobody (except the judges) have seen or heard yet: Siobhan Kelly from Northern Ireland and Alfie Hobbes from London.

Peter Kay, the legendary English comedian, comes into our holding room.

"Hi, Jamie. How are things?"

"You're Peter Kay!" I say (because I'm a huge fan).

He looks in the mirror. "Right you are. I am indeed. I'm also taking over the master of ceremonies gig. Hope you don't mind?"

"No, sir. I mean, I can't go onstage and introduce myself, right?"

"Well, you could. But you already know who you are, so what's the point?"

Finally, I start to relax. Like the doctors always told me, laughter is the best medicine—even for panic attacks. And Peter Kay is genuinely funny. He warms up by trying a few of his classic jokes out on Grace and me.

"I heard about these two Eskimos sitting in a kayak," he says. "They were chilly. But when they lit a fire in the boat, it sank, proving once and for all that you can't have your kayak and heat it, too."

"Mr. Kay?"

"Yes, Jamie?"

"You funny!"

"Thanks. Now let's just hope you are, too!"

chapter 43

FRIDAY NIGHT FRIGHTS

The semifinal round of the Planet's Funniest Kid Comic Worldwide contest airs live on Friday night (or what those of us in London call Saturday morning).

Viewers all over the world will get to vote by text, phone, and internet ballot. Their votes will be tabulated, and tomorrow, we'll all return to the Elstree Studios for the "live results" show.

I hate those. They'll make all sixteen contestants sweat it out and wait for two whole hours until, finally, at the very last minute, they announce the eight comics moving on to the live finals, which will take place on Monday night here. Then the eight finalists come back the next day for another two-hour sit-around-and-sweat fest, when the winner will be crowned. Not that there's actually a crown. Comedians don't wear tiaras. We make fun of them.

Peter Kay, our British master of ceremonies, opens the show with a very funny monologue.

"Welcome to the semifinals of the Planet's Funniest Kid Comic competition," he says to the camera that swoops down on a crane to greet him. The studio audience goes crazy. Spotlights swing up and down and all around. "I'm your host, Peter Kay. You know, this morning, I went to a restaurant that

Folks, I need to ask one question: What do people in China call their fancy plates?

serves breakfast at any time. So I ordered French toast during the Renaissance.

"Love being here with all these young comedians," says Kay. "When I was a child, I was the kid next door's imaginary friend."

The audience applauds.

One of the judges crosses his arms over his chest and scowls.

"Uh-oh," says Kay. "Milton looks miserable. No, wait. That's how he always looks."

"Can we please get on with the show?" grouses the mean judge, Milton Cromwell. "I suspect the young comedians will be far funnier than you, Peter."

"And I suppose they'll all look far more attractive than you, Milton!"

It might be a scripted bit, but I figure Joe Amodio must be happy up in the control booth. The show has just started and we already have enough conflict to start a small war.

I feel sorry for the Northern Irish comedian, Siobhan Kelly. She has to go on first!

"Good to be here," she says after Peter Kay introduces her. "I know what you're thinking. She's from Northern Ireland. She must know how to river dance. Are you nuts? You think I want to get my socks and shoes sopping wet dancing in the middle of a river? Oh, there's Milton Cromwell down there. I was going to give him a nasty look, but I see he already has one. Backstage, one of the other comedians came up to me and asked, 'How come whenever you ask an Irish person a question, they answer with another question?' 'Now why would you say that?' I asked him."

She earns a big round of applause.

The judges love her, too. Even Milton Cromwell.

"That took guts to insult me like that," he says. "Good for you, Siobhan."

"Wow," she says. "Coming from you, Milton, that means—absolutely nothing. Look, it's okay if you want to donate your brain to science. But you probably should've waited until after you died."

The crowd roars. Milton doubles over with laughter.

With the audience and judges going crazy for Siobhan's brand of insult comedy, I'm starting to wonder: maybe I should've worked some put-downs into my act, too.

Is my feel-good comedy going to feel...boring?

Chapter 44

TIME TO BREAK MY SOLEMN VOW?

Early on, I made a vow that I would never try to get laughs by making fun of someone else.

I mostly make fun of me. And my struggles. And what it's like to be a middle schooler seeing the world at butt level from my wheelchair.

But, it seems, the kids going onstage haven't promised themselves the same thing.

Gabriela Guarachi from Peru makes fun of her neighbors in Chile.

"I was sitting on the riverbank one night fishing on the Chilean border. Along came a Chilean on the opposite side. He sat down and began to fish. Later that night I was catching all sorts of fish. The

Chilean? Nothing. 'Hey, can I cross the river to fish with you?' I told him, 'Sure. There's a bridge a couple miles down the road.' 'That'll take too long,' he said. 'Well,' I told him, 'you could row a boat or swim over here.' 'I don't have a boat,' he told me. 'And I can't swim!' Finally, I said, 'Okay. I am going to shine my flashlight across the river—you can walk across on the beam of light.' The Chilean thought about that for a minute. Then he said, 'What, do you think I'm stupid? I know you Peruvians. Once I'm halfway across the river, you'll turn off the light!'"

The judges love her.

Zhou Yang, the Chinese comedian, makes fun of the Koreans.

"So, I asked my North Korean friend how his life was going. He said 'Can't complain.' Because, hello, nobody in North Korea is allowed to complain about anything!"

The studio audience and the judges love *him*, too!

Miguel from Mexico does his Day of the Dead bit again. I think it's hysterical. Milton Cromwell does not. He also doesn't like Jean-Claude Bernard, the French mime, who does another hysterical silent bit—this one about a guy who eats too much food...

on a rocky boat. Cromwell hates Ichika, too. In fact, he calls her "Good-bye Kitty."

Next up is Chiku Jemaiyo from Kenya.

"Did you hear about the very handsome man who was in a car accident?" Chiku asks the audience.

(I can relate. Except for the very handsome part.)

"The doctors save the handsome man's life, but he loses one eye. Before a nice glass one can be fitted, they give him a temporary wooden eye. The man becomes very depressed and sits at home, moping around. Eventually his friends come over and drag him out to a disco to try and cheer him up. One of his friends suggests he talk to a cute girl who's all alone. 'No, she'll never go for a man with a wooden eye,' he says. 'Okay,' says his friend, 'how about that girl over there? She has a really big nose. Maybe she'll dance with you.' The man summons up all his courage, walks over to the girl, and says, 'Would you like to dance?' The girl gets all excited. 'Would I?! Would I?!' she says. To which the man responds 'Big nose! Big nose!'"

The audience loves her.

Milton Cromwell? Not so much.

"That joke sounds like something you'd hear in fifth grade," he tells her. "Maybe you can win the Funniest Kid Comic in the Fifth Grade contest. But you certainly don't belong on this stage."

I want to roll out there and tell the judge he's wrong. But I'm stuck in the wings. My wheels locked.

"I smell your anger, Jamie," whispers Hamish. He's standing right next to me. He puts on a Yoda voice, if, you know, Yoda was from the planet of Australia. "Fear is the path to the dark side. Fear leads to anger. Anger leads to hate. Hate leads to suffering."

I laugh a little and calm down. Slightly.

I also fear for Hamish.

He's up next.

Chapter 45

FLYING BLIND

"**G**ood evening, ladies and gentlemen," says Hamish, starting his routine the way he always does. "If that's what you are. You could be sheep and cattle for all I know. In case you couldn't tell, I'm blind as a bat. Actually, I'm blinder. At least a bat has radar."

The audience laughs.

"Yeah, I'm blind. But so is love. Cupid's mother was right. She knew he'd put his eye out if he kept playing with those arrows. My girlfriend just broke up with me. She thinks we should see other people. I told her that's impossible. Of course, I can read Braille. Those bumpy letters. My friends tease me sometimes. They're always asking me to read their Legos. The blocks all say the same thing: 'Quit asking me to read your stupid toys, mate!'"

The crowd is loving him. Me too. And, so far, he hasn't made fun of anybody but himself.

"As you could tell from my accent, I'm from Australia," Hamish tells the crowd. "The land down under. Home of Greg Norman, of course— the world-famous golfer. I met Mr. Norman in Sydney once. Challenged him to a round of golf. 'You play golf?' he says, all surprised. 'Oh, yeah,'

I tell him. 'Been doing it for years.' 'But how can you play golf if you're blind?' he asks. 'Easy. I get my caddie to stand in the middle of the fairway and yell at me. I listen for the sound of his voice and play the ball toward him. Then when I get to where the ball lands, the caddie moves further down the fairway or to the green and, once again, I play the ball toward his voice.'

"'But how do you putt?' Greg Norman asks me. 'Well,' I tell him, 'I get my caddie to lie down in front of the hole and whistle. I just play the ball to where the whistle's coming from.' Now Greg Norman is amazed. He says, 'We should play sometime.' 'Well,' I tell him, 'people don't take me seriously so I only play for money. And I never play for less than one hundred thousand dollars a hole.' 'Fine,' says Norman. 'When do you want to play?' I shrug my shoulders and say, 'I don't care. Any night next week is fine by me.'"

The audience gives Hamish a standing ovation.

I'm so happy for my new friend. But as he's taking his bows, I look across the stage and see Joe Amodio talking to Suzannah Katris, the girl from Perth. Hamish's Australian teammate.

Mr. Amodio looks mad. He is pointing like crazy at Hamish.

Suzannah just nods. I think Mr. Amodio just gave our next comedian her marching orders.

While the audience cheers for him, Peter Kay escorts Hamish offstage, over to where Suzannah and Joe Amodio are standing. Peter then hustles back to center stage to introduce our next comic.

"Quick news bulletin before we bring out our next comedian," he says. "A cement mixer collided with a prison van on the Kingston Road. Motorists are asked to be on the lookout for sixteen hardened criminals. And now, let's hear some thunder for our second comic from down under...hailing from Perth, the edge of the world, give it up for Suzannah Katris!"

She comes onstage.

And starts ripping into Hamish!

KILLER COMICS

Wow.

Maybe Mr. Amodio is right. Maybe comedy is nothing more than a vicious blood sport. Suzannah, the Aussie queen of the two-liner joke, turns her set into a bout of pro wrestling—without the funny tights, masks, and body slams.

First, she makes fun of Hamish.

"You know," she says, "girls only call Hamish ugly until they find out how much money he has. Then they call him ugly and poor. Want to hear a word Hamish just made up? Plagiarism. He went to see a faith healer who said unto him, 'Come forth and you will regain your eyesight.' But Hamish came fifth and won a toaster."

Then she turns on me!

"I think Jamie Grimm, the wheelchair comic, stole my handbag." She shakes her fist in the air. "Grimm? You can hide but you can't run. I think he also stole my mood ring. I don't know how I feel about that."

Thankfully, the audience isn't laughing. They're in shock. Their jaws are hanging open. Mine, too.

What's Mr. Amodio up to? I wonder. After all, I'm the star of his biggest hit on the BNC network. I can feel my ears starting to burn. That's what happens when I get mad. Or if I park too close to a heat lamp.

Why would Joe Amodio send Suzannah onstage to trash Hamish and me, but none of the other comedians? Is he trying to drum up the sympathy vote for us, his two "disabled" comedians? If so, I don't want it. In fact, it makes me so *angry* to think he would—

Wait a minute.

I remember what Gilda told me: "*Joe Amodio is trying to knock you off balance. He loves conflict. The best TV for him would be for you to lose your cool and win by going negative. Don't give him what he wants.*"

I take a deep breath, close my eyes, and silently thank Gilda for sometimes knowing me better than I know myself.

I'm feeling calmer. My pulse isn't racing quite so fast.

In the spotlight, Suzannah is finishing up her insult spree.

"I don't know what makes Jamie Grimm so unfunny, but it sure is working. And Hamish? I don't know if he's always this stupid or if today is a special occasion."

The audience is actually booing her.

Peter Kay bounds onstage and grabs the microphone from her. Suzannah slouches off to the wings.

"You know," says Peter Kay, "I saw Suzannah at rehearsals yesterday. She was wearing a sweatshirt with 'Guess' on it. I said, 'Anger management issues?'"

The joke takes some of the tension out of the auditorium.

But I have a feeling it will be back soon. Peter Kay announces the next act.

"Now put your hands together for the funniest thing to come out of Russia since pickled mushrooms and meat Jell-O, the one and only Vasily Vasilovich!"

Chapter 47

VASILY THE VALIANT

Vasily marches onstage to his martial music.

"Thank you, Mr. Peter Kay. A very funny man, no? May I just say, I did not like how the little girl from Australia made fun of the other comedians. I did not like it at all. So I will do it much, much better."

The audience chuckles.

"Ichika, the comedian from Japan, she thinks she is funny. If I agreed with her, we'd both be wrong. And whatever kind of look she was going for, she missed. As you probably noticed, there are no German comedians here with us tonight. Big surprise. So, how many German comedians does it take to screw in a lightbulb? I will tell you. Zero. There is no such thing. A German may come to put in the light-bulb, but they can't be comedian because Germans are not funny. You are now permitted to laugh."

The audience obeys his orders. They laugh.

"Did you know that four out of five people suffer from diarrhea? Does that mean one person enjoys it? Most of the comedians in this competition are like that toy, the Slinky. They're not really good for anything, but you can't stop smiling when you see one tumble down the stairs. Jamie Greem? I'm thinking about you...

I told all the other comedians, "The last thing in the world I want to do is hurt you. But it's still on the list."

"I tell you, the Americans in this competition are not so bright. They both think that USB is a backup plan just in case USA fails. But America is not a very bright country. They choose from just two people for president but fifty for Miss America. You are now permitted to laugh. How about that Hamish Gadsby? The blind boy from Australia? Do not feel sorry for him, my friends. He is not as sweet as you might think. The other day, Hamish called me up and asked me if I ever got a shooting pain across my body. 'Like someone has a voodoo doll of you and they're sticking it with pins?' he said. 'No,' I told him. 'How about now?' he asked."

The audience is laughing louder.

"Miguel, the kid from Mexico, he is very smart. His routine was very, very clever. But I told him an ancient Russian proverb: 'Knowledge is knowing a tomato is a fruit. Wisdom is not putting it in a fruit salad.'"

I'm even chuckling a little. Vasily's dialed down his anger a few notches. Probably because he heard those boos Suzannah picked up with her slash-and-burn routine.

He saves his last joke for me.

"I must say, Jamie Greem may not be funny, but he certainly is brave. To come out here in a wheelchair, without any real jokes? That boy has the heart of a lion. And a lifetime ban at the zoo."

He doesn't have to do his catchphrase again.

The audience knows they have permission to laugh and they're doing it.

Chapter 48

JOKING NICE

I barely hear Peter Kay say my name when he does my introduction.

I am too busy focusing on what Gilda told me: *"Be who you are, not who they want you to be."*

I roll onto the stage and grab the microphone. The follow spot—blazing like a lighthouse beacon—blinds me. All I see is fuzzy whiteness and floating dust bunnies. But I know the audience is out there. I can hear them holding their breath while they wait to see if I still funny.

Like Hamish before me, I always like to address the elephant in the room before diving into my material. No, I don't say, "Hello, elephant." I go ahead and let the crowd know that, yes, I know I'm in a wheelchair.

"Hello, everybody. I'm Jamie Grimm. When people meet me, the first thing they want to know is 'How did you end up in a wheelchair?' So let's get that answered right away: I was in a car accident when I was about ten. And yes, I had no business driving at that age."

They laugh. I relax.

"Since I won the Planet's Funniest Kid Comic competition last year, a lot of companies have asked me to work their products into my routine. They said they'd actually pay me, just for mentioning their brand names. Well, to be honest with you, the whole idea of selling out like that just makes me sick to my stomach. That's why I rely on Pepto-Bismol... now available in chewable tablets. Yummy.

"This tour we've been on has been a lot of fun," I tell the crowd. "Of course, going around the world in a wheelchair isn't easy. That's why we used an airplane. But I've got to say, Berlin is one of the most wheelchair-accessible cities I've ever visited. I'm very glad they tore down that big wall they used to have right in the middle of town..."

The audience is chuckling. I switch into some non-wheelchair-specific material.

"The people I've met on this trip have been so nice. In Brazil, if you send someone a thank-you card, they'll send you back a 'you're welcome' note. In Australia, I saw a lady apologize to a mannequin she bumped into. People in Africa are so sweet, I think Willy Wonka is jealous. In Dubai, I met this really nice banker. He promised to lend me some money until I got back on my feet. I said he was nice, not smart."

I riff on the food I ate around the world. And the strange things different countries put into their sausages.

I talk about how hard it is for me to use the cramped toilet on an airplane, because there really aren't handicap bathrooms at thirty thousand feet, even on private jets. I end up contorted sideways in my chair with my eyes closed at the end of that bit.

"No matter where we traveled, I saw signs at the crosswalks. In all different languages. 'Push button. Wait to walk.' So I pushed the button and waited. And waited. And waited. None of those buttons worked…"

I end my time with a plea for everybody to take their troubles and turn them into opportunities.

"And," I say, wrapping up my set, "never make the same mistake twice. There are so many new ones, try a different one every day."

I think I did pretty well.

But, judging from the sour expression on his face, I doubt that Milton Cromwell agrees with me.

Chapter 49

BRIT WITS

"**O**h, good," says Cromwell. "You're finally finished. I've had trips to the dentist that were more fun than listening to you."

Ouch.

I tighten my cheeks and keep smiling. It hurts. But nobody (especially me) wants to see me weep on live TV.

"I'm sorry," says Cromwell over a few boos and groans from my fans in the audience, "but if I'm being honest, that was one of the worst stand-up routines I have ever heard. And yes, I know—you can't stand up. You've been telling us that for over a year.

"Frankly," Cromwell continues, "we're all a wee bit weary of your act, Jamie. We've seen it. In the American competition. On YouTube. On that dreadful sitcom you do. Well, *dreadful* isn't the right word. *Awful* probably is. Or *nauseating*."

To my left, off in the shadows, I can see the

silhouette of Mr. Amodio slicing his finger across his throat, telling the judge to knock it off. I guess he doesn't mind Mr. Cromwell tearing me apart but he doesn't want him going after my TV show, because Joe Amodio produces it!

"Others might disagree with me," Cromwell says, "but we all know the truth—nobody wants to hear nice jokes about nice people doing nice things. It's just boring!"

"Oh-kay," says Peter Kay, coming onstage and draping an arm over my shoulder. "Sounds like somebody fell out of the wrong side of the bed this morning. So, Jamie, do you know that look Milton Cromwell gets when he's happy?"

I shake my head.

"Yeah, me neither," says Kay, looking down at the judges' panel. "You know, Milton, you remind me of the bullies I knew at school."

Cromwell crosses his arms over his chest. "Is that so?"

"Yes indeed," says Kay. "They laughed at me and called me all kinds of terrible names. But one day I turned to my bullies and said—'Sticks and stones may break my bones but names will never hurt me,' and it worked! From there on, it was sticks and stones all the way."

The audience laughs and applauds and, hopefully, forgets half the mean stuff Milton Cromwell said about me.

"Well, thank you, Jamie," says Kay. "Time to bring on our next contestant, from right here in London. Please welcome to the stage the one and only Alfie Hobbes!"

I roll offstage as fast as I can. My palms, of course, are once again slick with flop sweat.

Hobbes sneers down at me as our paths cross.

"Loser," he mutters.

I park in the wings and prepare for the worst.

"Jamie Grimm?" says Hobbes. "That bloke is supposed to be the funniest kid comic on the planet? He's even dumber than he looks. The last time I saw a face like his, I fed it a banana. The guy is so lame..."

The audience is hissing him, but Hobbes keeps going.

"...he's one taco short of a combo platter.

Boo all you want. Maybe I'll try being nicer if you try being smarter.

"I kid about comedians like Jamie Grimm," he continues. "Why? Because they're not funny enough to kid about me. Jamie Grimm is so dumb, he can't even think without moving his lips. The other day, I hear he changed his mind. I wonder what he did with the diaper."

And on and on it goes.

He attacks and insults me with such dogged determination, the audience has a change of heart.

They start loving Alfie and (gulp) hating me!

Chapter 50

THE HITS KEEP ON COMING

I finally retreat backstage to the dressing rooms.

And find Mr. Amodio giving a twisted pep talk to the remaining comics.

"You hear Alfie Hobbes out there? He's slaying that audience! They love the way he's tearing into Jamie and Europe and the whole world. That's what comedy is all about. Making fun of stuff!"

He sees me roll into the room.

"Jamie? You bombed, baby. Bigly. Cromwell was right. Nobody comes to a comedy show to hear you kids say nice things about nice people. They want insults and put-downs. Joke-to-joke combat. So, the rest of you, the ones who haven't been on yet? Unleash the dogs of war. Give me your top-notch, grade-A killer material. Tear each other apart! Be ruthless!"

"I don't know about that, mate," says Hamish. "There's more to comedy than insults and put-downs…"

Mr. Amodio tells everybody to ignore him. "Hamish already had his chance. He blew it, too. Word of advice? Don't go out there and be like Hamish or Jamie or even Chiku. Be like Vasily and Alfie. Kill big!"

The rest of the comics listen to Mr. Amodio.

Even my American teammate, Grace Garner. She still cracks jokes cornier than the Iowa state fair, but by sort of shouting them, she makes them sound mean.

"You know how you kill vegetarian vampires?" she shouts. "WITH A STEAK TO THE HEART! Why can't you hear a pterodactyl go to the bathroom? BECAUSE THE *P* IS SILENT! Why can't a bicycle stand on its own? IT'S TWO TIRED!"

Yep. She's screaming the punch lines.

"Why was the little strawberry crying? BECAUSE HIS MOM WAS IN A JAM! What should you do when you see a spaceman? PARK YOUR CAR, MAN! What's the difference between ignorance and apathy? I DON'T KNOW AND I DON'T CARE!!!!"

When she's done, Demarco Coetzee from South Africa takes the stage and rants about—everything!

Zhou Yang, from China, demands another minute at the mic so he can complain about people in America getting tattoos with Chinese letters. "Learn what you are spelling, idiots. That squiggle on your arm? It says 'Beef with Broccoli!'"

In the dressing room, Alfie Hobbes and Vasily are gloating.

"You might've been the funniest kid comic in America," Alfie sniffs at me, "but you're too soft and squishy to conquer the world."

"Leave that to your betters," said Vasily. "Me."

"You mean me," says Alfie.

"No, I meant me. You are a British twit."

"And you're a Russian buffoon!"

They spend the rest of the evening tearing into each other.

Me? I just want to go back to the boardwalk on Long Beach, forget all about comedy, and find a career where people are nicer to each other.

Maybe something civilized, like ultimate cage fighting.

Chapter 51

GILDA CALLING

As the last comic (Fadi) is onstage making fun of the comic right before him (Benji), my phone vibrates.

It's Gilda. Video calling from America.

"Hey," I say dejectedly when her face brightens my screen.

"What the heck is going on over there?" she asks me.

"Oh, you know—just some good old-fashioned comedic mud wrestling. And I'm the mud."

"What's up with that?"

"It's Joe Amodio's idea," I tell her. "It's that stuff he's always saying about conflict. I think he told

Suzannah to insult me, and everyone else piled on the Jamie Hater bus."

"Well," says Gilda, "don't let him get to you. You were fantastic and funny. You don't need to worry."

"But what if we're wrong and Mr. Amodio is right? What if comedy isn't supposed to bring people together? What if it's really supposed to rip them apart? You heard the applause for the kids who were being nasty."

Onstage, Fadi says something about Benji. It gives me hope: "I'd really like to help the guy out."

But then comes the punch line.

"Which way did he come in?"

And Fadi doesn't stop there.

"Today at the hotel, Benji farted in the elevator. It was wrong on so many levels."

Uncle Frankie hops onto the video call.

"I've never seen anything like this," he says. "This competition you got going on over there reminds me of the notorious Yakima yo-yo tournament of 1982!"

"I love it!" shouts Stevie, jumping up behind Uncle Frankie. It looks like they're all at the diner, watching the show on the big-screen TV. "This is my kind of comedy contest! Roller Derby with jokes. One hit after another!"

Gilda comes back on the screen.

"Hang in there, Jamie," she says. "We're all going to vote for you!"

"Not me!" shouts Stevie. "I'm going with Vasily. Or Alfie. They're both awesome. I love the way they make fun of you. Hey, tell them that 'Crip from Cornball' thing I used to call you. They can use it. Free of charge."

Gilda rotates the phone so I don't have to see Stevie pumping his arm in the air while chanting "Va-si-ly, Va-si-ly!"

"You'll be one of the eight who makes it to the finals," Gilda assures me.

"I don't know if I want to..."

"Yes, you do."

"Not if the next show is going to be like this one," I say. "After all, do punching bags ever step up and volunteer for their job? I haven't seen one yet."

"Well," says Gilda, "it's up to you to make it be the way you want it to be."

"But Amodio—"

"Isn't the one onstage with a microphone in his hand. You are!"

The show's about to end, so I say good-bye to Long Beach—wishing I could climb into my smartphone and magically transport myself back home. Peter Kay wraps up our live broadcast by talking directly to the vast worldwide TV audience.

"Who's going to move on to the finals? Well, that's up to you! There's only eight slots, so every vote counts."

He spells out all the ways viewers can vote: phone calls, texts, online polls, the works.

"The eight comedians moving on to the final round will be announced tomorrow night, right here in another live broadcast. Those eight will then compete in the finals for the title of the Planet's Funniest Kid Comic. See you tomorrow!"

All the comics ride back to our hotel in the same minibus.

The ride, as you might imagine, is pretty quiet.

That'll happen after so many people have spent so much time making fun of each other.

Chapter 52

AND THE LOSER IS...

The next night, we load back into the bus and drive off to Elstree Studios for the live results show.

Those are never very interesting. They'll show clips of everybody's auditions, Peter Kay and a couple of other adult comedians will crack jokes, and then we'll all troop onstage for the dramatic elimination sequence.

Vasily and Alfie, rested and ready for more nasty put-downs, regale the bus with jokes about their favorite subject. Me.

"You know, when Jamie Greem gets married, he will be looking for a strong woman. Not one with convictions or spirit. One who is strong enough to carry him up steps."

Alfie laughs. So does Vasily.

Don't you hate it when comedians laugh at their own jokes?

Alfie jumps in and piles on. "After Jamie gets married and has a baby, think of all the money he'll save. He won't need to buy a pram!"

"What's a pram?" asks Vasily.

"A baby carriage! Jamie can just put the kid on his lap and ask his wife to push him around and talk behind his back some more!"

"Knock it off, you two blobheads," says Hamish.

"Aw, isn't that sweet?" says Alfie. "Hamish is leaping to Jamie's defense. Now that's what I call *blind* loyalty!"

Everybody else on the bus keeps quiet.

When we reach the studios, we head off to our separate dressing rooms.

"Don't let them get you down, mate," Hamish advises. "They're just a pair of bullies. Like the ones who switched the hair gel in the gymnasium locker room with shaving cream."

I look at him.

"Yeah," he says. "I did not see that coming, that's for sure. I headed back to class looking like a fruit pie topped with whipped cream."

His joke makes me feel a little better. I'm not totally alone.

It also makes me wonder again if, last night, I should've fought back against the bullies—onstage.

I'm super worried. Not just because I might lose my comedy championship. I'm afraid I might lose it to Vasily or Alfie. Maybe I should've given in to the Dark Side of the Comedy Force. Maybe I should've slung some insults and put-downs of my own for an easy path to the final eight.

But now it's too late.

The results show starts. The worldwide audience has another look at snippets clipped from our routines.

They also get to rehear some of the judges' reactions.

Like Milton Cromwell telling me how awful I am.

The only part of the show I like is when Peter Kay is doing his one-liners or making fun of the judges.

"The other night, I saw six men kicking and punching Milton Cromwell out in the parking lot. A lady friend said, 'Are you going to help?' I said, 'No, six should be enough.'"

I'd like to tell the same joke. About Vasily and Alfie.

That's when Gilda's voice rings in my ear. *"Don't let them get to you, Jamie. Be who you are, not who they want you to be."*

"I'll try," I say to myself with a sigh.

And then it's time to roll onstage for the big reveal.

We form a line across the stage, each comedian illuminated by an overhead spotlight.

The lights go out. Drums roll.

"The world has voted," says Peter Kay dramatically, stretching out every single, solitary, individual word. "And...the eight comedians... moving on...to the finals...are...in order of votes received...from most to least..."

And then he waits. And waits. They always milk this bit for a long, long time.

"Vasily Vasilovich from Russia!"

Vasily's spotlight pops back on. He gives the camera a triumphant arm pump.

"Jean-Claude Bernard from France!"

Peter Kay picks up the pace. Every time he says a name, their overhead light *WHUMP*s on.

"Chiku Jemaiyo from Kenya! Benji Yatzpan from Israel! Hamish Gadsby from Australia!"

Yes! My new friend made it.

"Ichika from Japan!" She squeals. There are only two spots left.

"Miguel Ángel Gonzalez from Mexico."

We're down to one. Sweat is dribbling out of my hair and into my ears.

Peter Kay flaps the note card he's been reading from.

"The last comedian moving on to the finals...
the one receiving the least number of votes...is..."

WHUMP!

A light comes on.

"Jamie Grimm!"

Chapter 53

DETHRONED?

Peter Kay tells everybody to tune in "tomorrow" for the final round.

"Can Jamie Grimm hold on to his title of the Planet's Funniest Kid Comic? Or will one of our lucky seven finalists dethrone him? And why do we call the toilet a throne? Would a king or queen really want to spend their whole day sitting on one? I don't think so. They'd end up with a wrinkled butt. Sweet dreams. See you tomorrow, when we'll crown the Planet's Funniest Kid Comic!"

He waves at the camera.

The audience applauds one more time.

The stage lights go dark.

"We're clear," I hear the tech director, Mr. Wetmore, call over the PA speakers. That means we're off the air. I sag in my chair, feeling drained.

"What a show," says Hamish. "I hope I never see anything like that again."

I wait for him to land a blind joke punch line. He doesn't.

"Vasily? Congratulations!" says Joe Amodio, bounding onstage, rubbing his hands together greedily. "You took the top spot, *bubelah*."

"Are you surprised?" sniffs the Russian, puffing up his chest. "I am funny. The funniest comedian—child or otherwise—on this or any other planet!"

"We'll see about that, mate," snaps Hamish.

"No. You will not. Because you cannot see. Oh, look. I made a Hamish joke. Here is another one. My mother is so mean, she made me read the waffle iron. See? It is so easy to be you. But hear me now—tonight your blind jokes may have earned you many seeempathy votes. But tomorrow? I will bury you. Jamie Greem, too!"

"Yummy," says Mr. Amodio. "Looking forward to the funeral, big guy. I'm only sad that the people of the world didn't reward Alfie for his genius rant."

"The world is full of blooming idiots," the British comic snarls.

238

"Other losers?" says Mr. Amodio. "Gather round. Join me and Alfie over here...."

The other comedians not moving on to the finals form a sad, shoulder-slumped cluster around our big-shot TV producer.

"You kids aren't going home."

"We get another shot?" asks Demarco Coetzee.

"No, kid. You lost. But I want you all sitting in the audience for tomorrow's final round. People will love to watch you sulk as you cope with the agony of defeat."

"What if we don't want to be there?" asks Fadi Hanania.

"Tough tinsel, kid. You signed a contract. For the next two nights, I own you."

Fadi shakes his head. "I should've made jokes about Benji and the Israelis…"

"Yes," says Mr. Amodio. "You should've. But you didn't. So, you lost."

He turns to face Jean-Claude, Chiku, Benji, Hamish, Ichika, Miguel, and me.

"Don't you seven make the same mistake."

Jean-Claude, the mime, hops into a fighting stance and starts twirling his fists round and round like an old-fashioned boxer.

"Bring it on, French fry," taunts Vasily. "Maybe tomorrow you might even try talking. Jokes are much better when people can hear them. All of you, take your best shots. They still won't be good enough. I came in first tonight, I will come in first tomorrow. Jamie Greem? Prepare to give your throne to me!"

Great. Now he wants my wheelchair, too.

Chapter 5½

FROWN TOWN BUS

Vasily climbs into a stretch limo with Mr. Amodio.

The two of them are whisked off to a very late (it's like four in the morning, London time) after-party to celebrate Vasily's stunning victory. They'll probably party down with British breakfast food, which includes mushrooms, baked beans, and grilled tomatoes. I'm not jealous about missing out on the "delicious" food Vasily will be enjoying.

I am, however, feeling slightly envious. After-show victory parties are what I used to go to. All the time.

Everybody else boards the bus for the ride back to our hotel. I, of course, am the last one on because I have to wait for the hydraulic lift. As I roll toward the handicap spot behind the driver, I study the faces of the other kid comedians.

The six other finalists are eyeballing each other suspiciously.

The eight losers look miserable.

Somebody needs to tell these guys a joke. Fast.
I hook up my chair to the anchor straps in the

handicap space. Hamish is in the seat right across the aisle.

"Everybody looks like their dogs just died," I whisper.

"I know," says Hamish. "I can smell the despair in the air. And, Jamie?"

"Yeah?"

"You really need to find a better deodorant."

I nod. Flop sweat. It isn't pretty, but it sure is smelly.

"I used to think that comedy could bring people together," I say with a sigh as the bus rumbles down the roadway. "That laughter could make people feel better. One of the comedians I studied, a guy named Victor Borge, used to say 'Laughter is the closest distance between two people.'"

"Not in Joe Amodio's world," says Hamish, shaking his head. "He likes it to be more like a sledgehammer on a chisel—splitting people apart."

All of a sudden, Jean-Claude, the silent mime from France (the guy nobody's ever heard speak before), starts shouting. "*Sacré bleu!* What is that disgusting, foul-smelling tub of mud you keep dipping carrot sticks into like a deranged bunny rabbit?"

"It's hummus, you *schmegegge*," snarls Benji Yatzpan.

"Give chickpeas a chance!" shouts Fadi Hanania.

"You know, Fadi," growls Suzannah, queen of the two-liners, "you're not completely useless. You can always serve as a bad example."

Zhou Yang starts screaming at Ichika in Chinese. She screams back in Japanese. Even Grace Garner, the corn popper from Iowa, is getting in on the act. "You know what they call lawn furniture in your country?" she says to Siobhan, the comic from Northern Ireland. "Patty O'Furniture!"

Siobhan just calls Grace a gobdaw, which, I think, is basically the same thing as a *schmegegge*.

"We need to do something!" I say to Hamish.

"No, mate. *You* do."

"Me? Why?"

He jerks a thumb over his shoulder at the bedlam in the back of the bus. "Making this lot simmer down and smile? 'S'truth, mate. That's a job for the funniest kid on the planet. And, until I hear otherwise tomorrow, that's still YOU!"

Chapter 55

BUS SONGS

Hamish is right. I'm still technically the funniest kid on the planet.

But he's wrong, too. It's not my job to bring this snarling, yelping pack of kids together.

That's because a job is something you *have* to do. This is something I *want* to do. I just don't know how to start making everyone be pals.

So I start singing. At the top of my lungs.

"*The wheels on the bus go round and round! Round and round!*"

People stop insulting each other so they can gawk at me.

I keep going.

"*Round and round! The wheels on the bus go round and round, all through the town!*"

Okay. I definitely have everybody's attention. They're staring at me in total silence.

"My parents used to sing that song to me when I was like two or three," I say. "And even though I couldn't talk very well, I wanted to say, 'Hello? What did you expect the wheels to do? They're *round*. Of course they go round and round. If they did anything else…if they floated or danced or went sideways… now, that would be something to sing about."

"And how about the windshield wipers?" says Hamish, picking up on my riff. "They go swish, swish, swish? Not on my bus, mate. They're so old, they usually went SCRAPE, SKROOOONCH, KERTHUNK…" He starts making all sorts of strange, funny noises. "But nothing rhymes with KERTHUNK, so you can't bloody sing about it, can you?"

"My parents made me sing a song about a happy, talking spoon!" says Ichika. She sings some annoying lyrics about Spoon Tan making everything yummy. "This is why I use chopsticks. I'm afraid of spoons. They may start singing at me and shoveling gross food into my face!"

People are starting to laugh now.

"And what's up with that 'row, row, row your boat' song?" asks Grace Garner. "How can life be a dream? You just keep rowing, gently down the stream, merrily, merrily—over and over. The boat never gets anywhere. You ask me, it's a nightmare. They should put down the oars, stop rowing, jump out of the boat, and swim…"

"And what about Frère Jacques?" says Jean-Claude in his thick French accent. "Why does the singer keep asking, 'are you sleeping, are you sleeping?' Is it really that hard to tell? Are Jacques's eyes closed? Is there drool on his pillow? If so, he's sleeping! And, by the way, if Frère Jacques wants to sleep, let him sleep. Enough with the din, din, don and the ding, ding, dong."

"Those morning bells are enough to make the babies on the bus go waa, waa, waa!" adds Chiku. "In Kenya, kids have to sing 'number one, two, three, four, five. Let us count again.' So we had to keep counting because the lyrics said 'let us count again.' Same numbers. One, two, three, four, five. *Namba moja, mbili, tatu, nne, tano.* None of us knew about the numbers six, seven, eight, or nine for years."

Now everybody is cracking up.

"Let's face it," says Alfie Hobbes. "Our parents are all bloomin' idjits!"

"But still," I say, waving my arms to conduct the choir, *"the wheels on the bus continue to go round and round, round and round."*

And everybody joins in. Pretty soon, we're changing the lyrics. Making them funnier.

Seeing everybody having fun, jamming with one another, building on their fellow comedians' jokes, gives me an idea.

And it isn't one Joe Amodio is going to like.

Chapter 56

BURGER TALK

The next afternoon, I invite the other finalists to my hotel room for a burger fest.

I'm guessing everybody slept in after the late-night semifinals round. Well, everybody except me. I was too busy worrying about my big plan to do much sleeping.

Around one-thirty, Jean-Claude, Chiku, Benji, Hamish, Ichika, and Miguel troop into my room.

"This is amazing," remarks Ichika, checking out the handicap-accessible bathroom. "There's no tub. The floor goes straight from the sink into the shower. You could dance in here."

"No," I deadpan. "I couldn't."

"Oh, he makes another wheelchair joke," says Vasily as he walks into the room, slowly clapping his hands together to give me mock applause. "He is so funny I forget to laugh."

Yes, I invited Vasily to this little confab, too.

Hey, if I truly believe in the power of comedy to bring people together, I have to include our Russian champion. He's a people, too. Maybe.

"I called room service," I announce. "They're sending up a bunch of burgers. Plus fries."

"You mean chips," says Hamish.

"Don't those come in a bag?" says Miguel.

"No, mate. Those are called crisps."

"I prefer *pommes frites*," says Jean-Claude. "We do not call them French fries in France. It would be, how you say, redundant."

"Like Japanese eggplant!" says Ichika. "Hello? It's just eggplant."

Everyone chuckles, enjoying the wisecracks.

Everyone except, of course, Vasily.

"Why are we having this meeting?" he asks.

"To work out a truce," I say. "For tonight's show."

Vasily arches a skeptical eyebrow. "A truce?"

"That's right, mate," says Hamish. "In the finals, we all agree that nobody attacks anybody else—no matter what Joe Amodio says."

I nod. "We all just tell our jokes, do our routines, and hope for the best."

Now Vasily laughs. Then he chortles, which is a kind of breathy, gurgly laugh. It's also annoying.

"Ah, ha, ha, ha. *Now* you are being funny, Jamie Greem. No insults? No put-downs? Give up what has made me the most admired comedian on the planet? I will do what I do best. I will destroy you." He starts pointing around the room at the other comics. "And you, and you, and you..."

He leaves the room. Chortling.

A bellhop rolls in a cart piled high with domed platters of burgers and fries.

And everybody starts joking about burgers. Ichika cracks a couple about special Japanese burger buns. "They're basically chewier rice cakes."

Pretty soon, we're all doing one-liners about condiments.

"A friend of mine rubbed ketchup in his eyes," says Miguel. "In Heinz sight, it wasn't a very good idea."

"Why is ketchup red?" I say, tossing out the setup.

"Because it saw the salad dressing," says Benji, landing the punch line and drumming a BA-DUM-DUM on his lap.

Pretty soon, we're all doing bits about zombies and penguins and parents and cell phones and driver's ed and everything else that makes kids in middle school laugh.

It's true. Comedy is something we all share, no matter what language we speak. It *can* unite us.

So, burgers devoured, we all agree that at the finals we won't attack each other. We'll show the world the unity a good laugh can bring!

But only if the tech director, Mr. Wetmore, agrees to play along.

Chapter 57

GILDA TO THE RESCUE

I don't call Mr. Wetmore.

Instead, I call Gilda and ask her to call him for me.

"I think it would be better coming from you," I tell her. "After all, you guys work together on *Jamie Funnie*."

"Um, so do you, Jamie," Gilda tells me. "That's why they call it *Jamie Funnie* instead of, I don't know, *Bob Funny*."

"But I'm a contestant. He's in charge of sending out the live show. It just seems weird for me to call him and ask for this favor."

"You're not asking for yourself, Jamie. You're doing this for everybody."

"Everybody except Vasily," I remind her.

"Right. He chortles a lot."

"You noticed that, too?"

"Yeah. On TV. He's one of those comedians who likes to laugh at his own jokes."

Gilda and I have a lot in common.

Finally, she agrees to call Mr. Wetmore.

Then we chat about how things are going back home in Long Beach.

"Pretty good. Uncle Frankie and Ms. Denning seem really happy together."

"How are things at the diner?"

"Back on track."

"Does anybody miss me? Any of the regular customers?"

"Yes. One in particular."

"Who? The guy who likes the George Carlin jokes?"

"Nope. Not him."

"Mr. Burdzecki?"

"Nope."

"Who, then?"

Gilda pauses. "Me."

My turn to pause. "I miss you, too."

"So hurry up, win this thing, and head home."

"Gilda?"

"Yeah?"

"Will you hate me if I don't win? What if I think it's more important that we show the world the power of comedy to bring people together? What if I have to lose to a loudmouth insult comedian to prove my point? Will you be disappointed?"

"Are you kidding? I'll be even crazier about you!"

It's so easy to talk to Gilda. It feels like something I could do for the rest of my life.

But first we have the live finals to get through.

I lay out my plan.

She hangs up and calls Mr. Wetmore.

I sit by the phone and dip a cold French fry into a tub of goopy mayonnaise. According to Jean-Claude, that's what they do in Belgium. Yum.

Gilda calls back. "Mr. Wetmore is on board," she tells me. "He'll do whatever we want. He hates Vasily, too. Nobody likes a chortler, Jamie."

"Mr. Wetmore could lose his job."

"He knows. Said he'll jump off that bridge when he comes to it. Plus, don't forget—*Jamie Funnie* is a huge hit for BNC TV. Bigger than this international comedy competition, which, hello, ends tonight."

"Well, the contest ends tonight, but the results won't be announced until tomorrow," I remind her.

"Okay. It's on for two more nights. *Jamie Funnie* could be on for twenty more years!"

"Seriously? I'd be in my thirties. We'd have to set the show in an old folks' home where I eat nothing but mashed potatoes and stewed prunes."

"Um, when you're in your thirties, you're not old. You're just getting started. You'll probably be building your own family with the one you love."

Gilda takes another pause.

I'm so glad we're not FaceTiming or on Skype.

I have a hot, flushed feeling that, thirty-five hundred miles from here in Long Beach, Gilda Gold is making goo-goo eyes at me.

THE LAUGHTER GAMES

That night, we're back at Elstree Studios for the finals.

The eight comics not performing are assigned seats in the auditorium. Down front. Where the TV cameras can catch their every reaction.

"Win it for Team USA, Jamie," says Grace Garner, giving me a high five. "I wish I were still in the competition. My boyfriend and I laugh about how competitive I am. But I laugh more."

She heads off to find her seat.

Joe Amodio comes backstage to meet with the eight kid comics still in the running. Ricky Gervais, the English comedian who starred in the original British version of *The Office* and became notorious for his insults and put-downs when he hosted the

Golden Globe Awards, is with Mr. Amodio.

"Okay, kids," says Mr. Amodio. "To put this thing on boil and watch it bubble out of the pot, Ricky here will be taking over for Peter Kay. He's an equal-opportunity offender."

Remember, kids— age and treachery will always triumph over youth and ability!

"I watched the semifinals," Gervais tells us. "Some of you are really smart. You know who you are. Some of you are really thick. Unfortunately, you don't know who you are. Just accept that some days you are the pigeon and some days you are the statue."

"Keep it bitter, Ricky," says Mr. Amodio before he turns to address the performers. "This is it, baby cakes. The finals. There's no holding back. Go out there and kill big. This is *The Hunger Games*—but with jokes instead of bows and arrows."

"One last thing," says Gervais. "Where there's a will, there's a relative!"

Mr. Wetmore's voice booms over the PA speakers.

"Places, everyone. We're live in five. Ichika? You're up first in round one."

For these finals, each comedian will do two sets of material. Viewers can start voting for their favorites as soon as the show goes on the air.

Five minutes later, the music swells, the lights swirl, and Ricky Gervais takes the stage. He immediately starts insulting the judge, Milton Cromwell. Milton Cromwell starts insulting Ricky Gervais.

"Oh, goody," I hear Vasily chortle behind me. "This is going to be my kind of show."

After a few more insults are exchanged, Gervais asks the audience to "give it up" for Ichika: "The best thing to come out of Japan since Pokémon and Toyotas!"

"Okay, Ichika," Mr. Amodio coaches our Japanese finalist, nudging her onstage. "Go out there and slay that audience! Insult somebody!"

Ichika looks at me.

And winks.

She goes onstage and does her "Hello Kitty" bit. It's still pretty funny. Especially when she talks about Hello Kitty Soy Sauce. "It's not salty. It's sweeeeeet."

Then she tells us how vending machines are everywhere in Japan. "There's five million of them. And they don't just dispense soft drinks, candy, and flying fish soup. You can also buy bananas in vending machines. Umbrellas, eggs, and ramen noodles. This dress? Straight from a vending machine. I call it my B-34 look…"

She doesn't make fun of anybody except herself and she still earns a ton of applause.

So far, my plan is working.

Chapter 59

FUNNY BUSINESS

Hamish is on right after Ichika.

He stays true to form and makes fun of himself and his way of *not* seeing the world.

"They say love is blind, but marriage is a real eye-opener. And then there's this bloke in Australia who wants all the blind folks to put spiky nails at the tips of our white canes. Thinks we could help out with his antilitter crusade. You know, Steven Wright, the famous American comedian, once wondered, 'If blind people wear dark glasses, why don't deaf people wear earmuffs?' Hey, I only wear dark glasses because they make me look cool. Like maybe I could sing the blues."

The audience is laughing. Off in the wings, Joe Amodio is fuming.

"I wish I could've brought my Seeing Eye dog onstage with me," Hamish continues.

The audience goes "Awwwww."

"Yeah. That's why I left him at home. You lot would've voted for him instead of me. But before I left Sydney, my dog and I went into a Mickey D's. I started swinging the dog around by his leash. The manager came running out. 'What do you think you're doing, young man?' he shouted. 'Just having a look around.' By the way, despite what you might've heard, it's quite easy to drive when you're blind. You just need to know the basics: keep one hand on the wheel, the other on the road."

Hamish earns a standing ovation from everybody except Milton Cromwell.

Benji Yatzpan spends most of his time making jokes about Jewish mothers.

"A man is lying on the operating table, about to be operated on by his son, the surgeon. The father looks up and says, 'Son, remember—if anything happens to me, your mother is coming to live with you.' Of course the surgery goes perfectly... I tell you, my mother doesn't just enjoy guilt trips. She runs the travel agency."

The audience loves Benji's routine but, once again, Milton Cromwell does not.

"What's wrong with you children?" he wonders aloud when Benji faces the judges' panel. "You're from Israel. You could've made fun of all those enemies you have in the Middle East. Instead, you made jokes about your mother, your bar mitzvah, and matzo ball soup."

Ricky Gervais actually turns on Milton Cromwell. "I thought the kid was funny," he says.

Jean-Claude Bernard goes on and does another hysterical wordless bit. This time it's a heroic sword battle with a dragon on one side and a mouse on the other! Miguel Ángel Gonzalez puts on his skeleton costume and does another superfunny Day of the Dead routine. Chiku Jemaiyo, from Kenya, is so hilarious, fresh, and uplifting, it makes Milton Cromwell and Mr. Amodio both turn totally purple with rage.

Only two comedians haven't done their first sets yet.

Vasily.

And me.

And I have to go on before him.

Chapter 60

I HOPE I FUNNY

Ricky Gervais takes the mic at center stage.

"We're almost to the end of the first round," he says. "For those of you watching in America or Australia or wherever—I'm from a little place called England. We used to run the world before you guys came along. And now, here he is, the reigning king of kid comedy, Jamie Grimm!"

The audience cheers, but all I can hear are the muffled voices inside my head. There's mine, the one that sounds all panicky and terrified. And then there's Gilda's. And Uncle Frankie's. I can even hear a little bit of Cool Girl coming through.

They're all reminding me to be myself. To stay true to who I am. They tell me, "I Funny."

This is my second-to-last performance in front of a worldwide audience numbering in the millions. Viewers are already voting. Mr. Amodio has a running tote board up on a computer monitor backstage. Believe it or not, I'm already in the top three. I think the gang back home in Long Beach is maxing out their votes like crazy.

Of course, I also saw who's in the number one slot: Vasily Vasilovich. And he hasn't performed tonight, either.

I take in a deep breath, remember the plan, and give it my best shot.

"Hiya, folks. I'm Jamie Grimm. The stand-up comedian who can't stand up. If I tried, I think I'd just fall down, and who wants to see a fall-down comedian? Kind of hard to talk into the microphone when you're lying facedown on the floor."

The audience is laughing. Milton Cromwell is scowling.

I roll into some of my classic zombie material.

"The real reason I'm in this chair? To escape the zombie apocalypse." I put on my best monster voice. "Let that morsel go. He has wheels. I don't want to chase after him. I am dead tired."

I try out some new material, too.

"Guys in wheelchairs, we don't really have super-heroes to look up to. I mean, sure, we've got Professor Xavier from the X-Men comics. And years ago, way back in the 1960s, there was the Doom Patrol, with the Chief, who had all sorts of weapons, including flamethrowers, built into his wheelchair. But that series died. I think it's time for Marvel or DC to introduce a new superhero. Chairman! It could be me, in a suit and tie. And I'd live in suburbia...because that's where chairmen and CEOs always live. I'd lead the superheroes of suburbia. Garbageman. Fireman. Paperboy..."

The audience is cracking up. Probably because I strike some pretty funny poses for each superhero. And Garbageman swats away a lot of flies.

"One last word of advice: Never criticize your girlfriend's choices. You're one of them. I'm Jamie Grimm! See you folks later!"

I give a jaunty wave. The lights come up.

I'm ready to face the judges.

Only I don't get the chance.

"Give me that microphone, Jamie Greem."

It's Vasily, shaking his head in disgust.

"After that lame set, we do not need to hear from the judges. We all know the truth…You not funny."

Chapter 61

KILLER MATERIAL

I roll offstage as quickly and as quietly as I can.

I wish I could just disappear.

But Vasily keeps ripping into me and my routine.

"Jamie Greem's life is so, so sad. But does he have to make us sad, too? Hurry home, little loser. You are depriving your village of its idiot. Some drink from the fountain of funny. Jamie Greem? He gargled and spit it out. I don't know where he got his looks, but I hope he kept the receipt."

I park in the wings with the other comics.

"He's a nasty piece of work," says Chiku.

"But he's in the lead," says Benji, gesturing toward the computer monitor where the votes are being tallied.

271

Vasily is still in first place. But, surprisingly, I'm in second!

I guess the worldwide audience liked my material better than Vasily did.

"Hey, Jamie!" says Ichika, batting her eyes at me. "You and Vasily are running away with this. The way I wish I could run away with you."

Yes, she's still flirting with me.

"Sorry. I can't run away with anyone," I tell her as I check out the vote totals pouring in from all around the globe. Ichika is correct. Vasily is only a few thousand votes ahead of me. But I'm almost ninety thousand votes away from Jean-Claude, the mime, who's in third.

Meanwhile, Vasily is still tearing me down onstage.

"Jamie Greem is a few clowns short of a circus. He is proof that evolution can go in reverse. Heh heh. Jamie Greem reminds me of a dog I knew with no legs. He didn't have a name, because even if you called him, he wouldn't come to you." Vasily grinned as the audience laughed. "Right now Jamie is backstage crying from all my jokes about him. I told him to insult me back, but he can't stand up for himself. Heh heh. You are now permitted to laugh."

When Vasily is (finally) finished roasting me, he moves on to the other comedians.

"I can't wait to hear Miguel Ángel Gonzalez again," he says with a yawn. "I could use the sleep. Hey, Miguel—can I take your picture later? I want to use it to scare my little sister. Then there is the mime, Jean-Claude. He is a performer of rare talent. It is rare when he shows any. Chiku, the chirpy girl from Kenya? If ignorance is bliss, she must be the happiest person in the world. Hamish? I hear he talked to his plants and they died of boredom. Benji Yatzpan? His clothes definitely make a statement. Too bad that statement is 'I have no taste.' You don't need a garment bag, Benji. You need a garbage bag. Who is left? Ah, yes. Our Japanese flower, Ichika. It must give you a great sense of power, Ichika, to know you could bore the world to death. And don't worry, if your mind wanders, it won't get far."

When he's done trashing the other comedians, he goes to work on the judges. "Milton Cromwell is so old his teeth are like the stars. They come out at night."

And on and on he goes. Vasily is chortling at his own jokes. The studio audience is laughing.

So, apparently, is the audience at home.

Because when Vasily finally comes off the stage at the end of the first round, he's ahead of me by more than one hundred thousand votes!

Chapter 62

COMMERCIAL BREAK?

"**W**e're in commercials," Mr. Wetmore announces from his perch in the control booth. "We're back in four minutes. Live!"

"Prepare for the second round," fumes Mr. Amodio. "And would at least one of you try to be as mean and nasty as Vasily? Hamish? It's obviously working for him and not so much for any of you. Check this out!"

The angry producer taps on the computer screen.

"Sounds like a birdie knocking on a window," deadpans Hamish.

"Look at this vote tally, kid."

Hamish whacks Mr. Amodio in the shin with his white cane. "Have you been paying attention to anything I've said, mate?"

"Fine. You're blind. I'll read you the numbers. Vasily is in the lead by one hundred and ten thousand votes. Jamie Grimm is in second. You're way down in fifth place. Why are you letting Jamie steal all your sympathy votes, Hamish? They could be yours. Just go out there and tear into him the way Vasily just did."

"But do not steal my material!" growls the Russian. "I still have a second set and will continue to demolish the Greem joker. Now get out of my way. I must go practice my scowl in the mirror."

He stomps off to the dressing rooms. Chortling.

Joe Amodio puts his hands on top of Hamish's shoulders. "Let me drop this in the pool and see if it makes a splash, Hamish: You can beat Jamie Grimm!"

"Um, you guys?" I say. "I'm sitting right here."

"We see you, *bubelah*," says Mr. Amodio. "But all's fair in love and war. I need conflict to make tonight's ratings soar. I also need a fresh new face for my next sitcom hit. It could be Vasily. Or it could be you, Hamish. You started out so strong, down in Sydney. Why do you think I picked you, out of all the contestants, to be the show's tour guide?"

"Because I was blind and people could describe stuff to me?"

"Wrong-o. I did it because I saw potential. I have an idea for a show built around you, kiddo: *Hamish Ha-Ha!*"

I hold up my hand like we're in school. "Um, Jacky Hart from *Saturday Night Live* is sort of using that title already."

"I'll buy it from her."

"We're back in sixty seconds," Mr. Wetmore calls over the intercom.

Mr. Amodio whips a walkie-talkie off his belt.

"I'm changing the running order for the second round, Richard," he barks into the walkie. "Hamish Gadsby will be up first."

"Got it," Mr. Wetmore answers back.

Mr. Amodio turns Hamish around and points him to the stage.

"Get out there, kid. And remember—this could be your big break! You may not win the competition, but you can definitely win my heart. Or my thumbs-up on your own show."

Hamish nods. I know he'd be terrific if he had his own show. He probably knows it, too.

The music starts up again.

Ricky Gervais is back at center stage.

"Time for the second round, ladies and gentlemen. Remember, you can vote up to ten times for your favorite comedian. Other than me, of course. You can vote for me a billion times. I'd like that. Now let's bring back the comic wonder from down under. Hamish Gadsby!"

Hamish taps his way onstage.

He seems very eager to get to the microphone.

Where he'll probably audition for his new sitcom by destroying me!

Chapter 63

HAMISH'S BIG MOMENT

I watch Hamish grip the microphone.

"Wow, I get to do two performances in front of the same audience," he says, cocking his head slightly to the right. "Wait a minute. Are you the same audience? Or did the daggy dills running this show switch everybody out when I wasn't looking?— which, by the way, is all the time."

The audience laughs.

"It's still us!" somebody yells.

"Thank you, sir. Or ma'am. With that voice, I couldn't really tell…"

I watch him take in a deep breath. Like he's getting ready to launch into his big bit. The one that's a hit job on me.

And then he doesn't.

280

"So, a blind kid walks into a restaurant," he says. "And a table. And a door. And this waiter carrying a huge tray of dirty dishes. It's not a pretty sight. Or so I've been told. By the way, does anybody know what you call a blind rabbit sitting on your face? An unsightly facial hare."

He keeps doing his usual material. The audience keeps laughing.

"A woman was taking a bath when she heard her doorbell ring. 'Who is it?' she called out. 'Blind man' was the answer. 'I'll be right there.' So, thinking a blind man won't notice that she's naked, she climbs out of the tub and doesn't even put on her robe. She opens the front door and the very surprised man on the front porch says, 'So, uh, where do you want these venetian blinds?'"

"What's he doing?" I hear Mr. Amodio hiss.

He grabs the walkie-talkie clipped to his belt. "Richard? Go to another commercial."

"Can't," Mr. Wetmore's voice crackles back. "Hamish is onstage. The kid's hysterical. You ever think of giving him his own sitcom? It could run right after Jamie's and—"

"Cut the feed, Wetmore!"

"And deny the world the comedic stylings of Hamish Gadsby? Sorry, sir. No can do."

"I'll can you!"

"Sorry, Joe. Can't hear you. I think the battery in my walkie-talkie is dying."

"You're fired!"

Mr. Wetmore doesn't respond. He also doesn't cut the live feed. And he's locked the control room door. That was part of the plan he and Gilda worked out.

I steal a glance at the tote board. Hamish is racking up the votes. So am I. Vasily? He's holding steady, but his lead is shrinking.

Meanwhile, a frantic Mr. Amodio uses a thick marker to write "CUT TO COMMERCIAL" in big bold letters across a cue card. He runs into the aisle and holds it up while hopping up and down with rage so Mr. Wetmore can see it in the booth.

Mr. Wetmore ignores him. The show keeps going out live to millions around the world. Hamish's vote tally keeps climbing.

Frustrated and trying to stay off camera, Mr. Amodio sneaks around the dark edge of the stage, tiptoes down the stairs, and whispers something into Milton Cromwell's ear.

Cromwell nods to whatever Mr. Amodio is telling him and bops his red buzzer button.

The SKRONK startles Hamish into silence.

"That will be enough, Mr. Gadsby," says Cromwell. "We don't need to hear you finish. I've just been informed that we're changing the rules of this competition."

Chapter 6½

NEW RULES

Ricky Gervais, the show's host, comes to center stage flapping a sheet of paper that Joe Amodio just scribbled something on.

"Sorry about this, Hamish," he says. "Looks like we're changing the rules in the middle of the game. Nobody saw it coming."

"Lovely," cracks Hamish. "For once I'm not alone."

"Righty-o. Good-bye, Hamish. I have to do something I'm probably going to regret in the morning."

He waves the sheet of paper.

Hamish, shoulders slumped, taps his way offstage, wondering, like the rest of us, what the heck is going on.

"Milton?" Gervais says to the judge. "According to this note I was recently handed, I'm supposed to turn this over to you. So, against my better judgment, I am doing as I have been instructed."

"Thank you, Ricky," says the judge.

The cameras spin around to frame him up. Cromwell smiles. It looks like his face might splinter.

"As you know," he says into the lens, "people all over the world have been voting for their favorite comedians ever since we went on the air. However, it has come to the attention of our producers that there are two clear favorites. In fact, there are only two comedians with a mathematical chance of being named the Planet's Funniest Kid Comic. Jamie Grimm is one of the leaders, thanks in part to the *Jamie Funnie* marathon that aired on BNC's global network all day today, as well as his status as the reigning champion. The other contender is our current leader, Vasily Vasilovich from Russia."

"What about Hamish?" asks Gervais. "The kid's funny. So are all the other contestants."

"The numbers have spoken."

"Fine," says Gervais. "But I think it's bloody unfair to ruin these kids' hopes before the votes are all in. Now I've spoken. And I also quit."

He drops the mic and strolls offstage.

Yeah. This sort of thing can happen on live TV.

"You're being very rude, Ricky!" Cromwell calls after him.

Gervais laughs. "If only I had a dollar for every time someone's said that. Oh, wait. I do. Ta!"

He's gone.

"Now can we puh-leeze cut to a commercial?" Joe Amodio shouts up to the booth.

And this time, Mr. Wetmore listens. Because nobody really wants to watch a TV show featuring an empty stage and a microphone stand.

A graphic stating WE'LL BE RIGHT BACK floats across the screen. Music swells. And the world gets to watch another commercial.

Mr. Amodio and Milton Cromwell huddle at the judges' table.

"Fine," says Cromwell. "I'll do it."

He marches onstage and grabs the microphone off the floor.

"Ladies and gentlemen," he says to the studio audience, "due to Mr. Gervais's recent temper tantrum and unexpected departure, I will be your new master of ceremonies. We'll be on the air in sixty seconds. Here's how this is going to work. To make the show even more exciting, we're saying good-bye to all but two of our contestants."

The audience—especially the fans of Hamish, Jean-Claude, Chiku, Benji, Miguel, and Ichika—boo loudly. Some even shout insults at Cromwell, which he probably would appreciate under different circumstances.

"Allow me to finish, please," says Cromwell, sounding crankier than usual. "As I said, the producers ran the numbers. None of the six other comedians stood a chance of catching up with the leaders of the pack. So, this will be a sudden-death joke-off. Jamie Grimm versus Vasily Vasilovich. We'll flip a coin to see who goes first."

I turn to Hamish, who is standing next to my chair.

"I'm so sorry…" I say.

"No worries, mate. But, Jamie…"

"Yeah?"

"Promise me one thing."

"What's that?"

"Tear Vasily apart. And while you're at it, knock Mr. Amodio down a few pegs, too!"

Chapter 65

THE JOKES ARE ALL ON ME

We're back on the air.

Milton Cromwell is in the spotlight at center stage.

"Vasily? Jamie? Please join me onstage."

I roll out from the stage-right wings. Vasily marches on from stage left. We meet in the middle.

"Congratulations," says Cromwell. "You're our two leaders and the only two comics still standing."

I don't take the bait.

"Our esteemed and enlightened producers have decided to cut to the chase," Cromwell continues. "We're going into a one-on-one, sudden-death joke-off. You will each get five minutes to do your best material."

"Who goes first?" grunts Vasily.

"We'll soon see," says Cromwell, pulling out an oversized coin. "Jamie, you are the current champion."

"Only for a few more minutes," scoffs Vasily.

"Therefore," says Cromwell, sniggering at Vasily's little dig, "we will let the challenger, Vasily Vasilovich, call the coin toss."

Cromwell flips the coin into the air.

"Heads!" shouts Vasily.

The coin clunks on the floorboards.

"Heads it is," says Cromwell. "You're up first."

"*Horosho,*" says Vasily. I think that's the Russian word for "good." But it sure sounds like *horror show*, which is what I might be in for.

I roll offstage.

And before I even reach the wings, Vasily grabs the microphone and starts ripping me to shreds.

"Look at poor leetle Jamie Greem. Pumping his way offstage. Boo-hoo. He is still trying to win the seeempathy vote because he is lame. This must be why his jokes are so lame. But let's not make fun of his comedy act. Why should we? There is so much more to make fun of. God made rivers, God made lakes. God made Jamie; we all make mistakes."

289

The audience laughs, but not as loudly as they did during Vasily's first set. The guy is such a bully, meanness oozes out of his pores the way BO oozes out of mine.

"And, Jamie?" he calls offstage. "Do yourself a favor and ignore anyone who tells you to be yourself. Bad idea in your case."

Then Vasily goes someplace even nastier.

But, please, Jamie, don't hate me because I am so handsome. Hate me because your girlfriend thinks so, too.

I could stir a bowl of alphabet soup and write better jokes than the ones you come up with

Jamie, are you always such an idiot or do you just show off when I'm around?

He starts making fun of my parents.

"Your mother and father are living proof that two wrongs don't make a right."

Anger and rage and hate boil my blood and turn my ears lobster red.

My mother and father can't be living proof of anything. They both died in the car wreck that put me in my chair.

"Jamie's mother is so dumb, when the family was driving to Disneyland, she saw a sign that said DISNEYLAND—LEFT so she went home. She's so dumb, she climbed over a glass wall to see what was on the other side. She's so ugly, when she tried to enter an ugly contest they said, 'Sorry, no professionals.'"

Now my blood pressure is so high, I can hear my heart throbbing inside my ears.

Next, Vasily makes some more horrible jokes about my father. Then he goes way too far.

"Jamie Greem's sister was so ugly when she was born, his mother said, 'What a treasure!' And his dad said, 'Let's bury it in the backyard.'"

Nobody is laughing.

Especially not me.

My little sister, Jenny, died in that car crash, too.

THE LAST WORDS

Milton Cromwell takes center stage as Vasily marches off to a smattering of applause.

The audience looks shocked. Me? I'm fuming, furious, and frothing for revenge.

"Wow, that was smashing," says Cromwell, smirking. "As in you totally destroyed, clobbered, and smashed your competition. Let's see if Jamie Grimm fires back. Here he is, ladies and gentleman, the current—and maybe former—funniest kid on the planet, Jamie Grimm!"

I don't think I've ever pumped my wheels harder. Anger and adrenaline are shooting through me like a Big-Gulp-with-Orange-Hostess-Cupcakes sugar rush. I am going out there, all alone, to demolish Vasily Vasilovich. It's just me against him. One on one. Mano a mano. Insult-o a insult-o.

No one can say things like that about my family and get away with it! I'm about to show Vasily what real insults are like. No one he loves or even likes will be safe from my "humor."

But then, when I've rolled, enraged, about halfway across the stage, a song the late Jerry Lewis used to sing at the end of his annual Labor Day telethon (yes, some of the VHS cassettes at the Hope Trust Children's Rehabilitation Center were antiques) starts ear-worming its way into my brain:

> *Walk on, with hope in your heart*
> *and you'll never walk alone.*

That's me.

Not the walking part. But on my incredible journey, which has, for the most part, been filled with incredible humor and hope, I remember I was never, ever on my own. Even during the darkest days right after the car crash happened...other people were always right there with me.

Right away there were all the first responders, doctors, nurses, and therapists who helped me pull my life back together after that tragic, rain-slicked night on the highway.

And I can't forget all the classic comedians, including Jerry Lewis, who made me laugh when I was in a full-body cast and thought all I would ever do again was cry.

Then there's my family. The Smileys. Uncle Frankie and New Aunt Flora. And all the customers at the diner who laughed at my jokes before I even thought about telling some onstage.

I can't forget my friends at school, either. Gaynor and Pierce. They stood by me, through thick and thin. Even cornball Vincent O'Neil. And what about Cool Girl? She was always there to talk to me even when I didn't know I needed someone to talk to.

And, of course, at the top of the list, there's Gilda Gold.

Gilda's with me wherever I go. Always reminding me to be myself. Her words constantly echoing inside my thick skull: *"Don't let them get to you, Jamie. Be who you are, not who they want you to be."*

Of course, my mind also hears a few words from cousin Stevie. *"Give that Russian dude a word wedgie, cuz!"*

I reach center stage, wiggle the microphone free from the stand, and decide to listen to the biggest and best voice in my head.

Gilda. Not Stevie.

"Thank you, Milton. Good to be back for round two. Ouch. This microphone is still sizzling from where Vasily scorched me. But he missed a few easy shots. For instance, this haircut. Check it out. Incredible what you can do with a bowl and a pair of scissors, am I right?"

I smile widely. The crowd laughs. Vasily Vasilovich will not have the last word about "Jamie *Greem*." And he won't force me to be something I don't want to be—a nasty, insulting comic just like him. Because I can make fun of myself better than anybody on this or any other planet.

Making jokes at your own expense?

Sometimes it's the most fun you can have sitting down.

Chapter 67

LAUGHING AT MYSELF

"**H**ey, folks, if you were going to vote for me out of sympathy," I continue, "please don't. My life's pretty great. I've got good friends, a fantastic family, and a comfy seat wherever I go. 'I'm sorry, sir, the concert is all sold out. There are no more seats in the auditorium.' That's okay. I've got my own."

The audience is really with me.

"Now, I know what you're thinking. Vasily should be ashamed of himself, making fun of a kid in a wheelchair. After all, I can't stand up for myself. But don't you worry, I'm doing fine. Seeing more butts than I'd like, but other than that, fine. I even tried out for the Paralympics. Came home all bruised and battered. That'll teach me to enter the hurdles. Should've stuck with pole vaulting...I may not be the brightest crayon in the toolshed, but at least I'm also terrible at making analogies.

"The biggest problem about being stuck in a wheel-chair? You're never quite sure why people like you. It can be confusing. Do they like me or do they like my handicap parking placard? 'Hey, let's go to the movies with Jamie! We can park right at the curb.'

"It's even worse with girls. You know how it is in middle school. One of your friends tells you that one of their friends heard that one of her friends likes you. It's so complicated. Romance is like that. No matter how old you are. I heard this husband and wife arguing the other day. 'You know,' he said, 'I was a fool when I married you.' She said, 'Yes, dear. But I was in love and didn't notice.' So what am I, Jamie Grimm, looking for in a girl?"

I look at the camera and hope Gilda can see the twinkle in my eye, because she, basically, put it there.

"Nothing. I'm not really looking, because I think I already found her. I just need to tell her how terrific she is. Which I will do later tonight when I give her a call. You know, that's something we should all do. Quit using your phones to cast votes in this competition. Call somebody you love and let them

298

know about it. Do it tonight. Or today, depending on your time zone. Hey to everybody back home in Long Beach. I love you guys. I can't wait to come home—where normal is just a setting on the dryer."

I'm Jamie Grimm. Even if it's over, it's been a fun ride!

While the audience cheers, I look up toward the bright lights hanging from a grid thirty feet above my head.

I love you guys, too. I say it silently.

But I know Mom, Dad, and Jenny hear me.

Chapter 68

THE WINNER IS...

I, of course, call Gilda and the gang as soon as the show is over.

"You were awesome!" she tells me. "You probably won't win, but that doesn't matter. You were awesome!"

"Thanks," I tell her. "And to tell you the truth, I really don't care if I win or lose. I just want to come home and make silly movies with you."

"Um, what about our network television show?"

"Okay. We can work on that, too."

Uncle Frankie grabs the phone from Gilda. "Your mom and I are so proud of you, kiddo!"

For a second, I wonder if he read my mind when I looked up into the rafters and said my silent prayer. And then I remember: He and Ms. Denning are married and want to adopt me. They're my new mom and dad.

"Did the adoption papers go through?" I ask.

"Like a hot yo-yo through a tub of butter! Welcome to your new family, Jamie."

I'm feeling pretty great the next night when we all bus back to the studio for our final results show.

"Very sneaky move," says Vasily when he sees me in the wings. "Getting all mushy like that. But it will not work. I will still win."

I just shrug. I don't really care.

"Last night's ratings were through the roof!" Joe Amodio tells me. "Especially when you went on, Jamie baby. People started texting their friends, calling their mothers, tweeting about it. You were trending like crazy, kiddo. That's why I love you. Always have. Always will. You understand comedy. When it needs a little schmaltz on top. Can't wait to get back to shooting *Jamie Funnie* with you and Gilda. She's your girlfriend, huh? Sweet. Gotta run. We'll talk."

No, we won't. Because Mr. Amodio never lets anybody get a word in edgewise.

Peter Kay is back as our host for the results show.

He does a few funny monologues, imitates Milton Cromwell's attempts to emcee a live TV show (it's hysterical—he keeps talking to the wrong cameras), and introduces clips about last night's drama, confusion, and comedy.

"I watched it all at home," says Kay. "Got a little hungry and called up a takeout restaurant. 'Do you deliver?' I asked. 'No,' they told me. 'We do lamb, chicken, or fish.' Anyway, it's time to announce our winner. Either that or I'm having amnesia and déjà vu at the same time. I think I've forgotten this before. Jamie? Vasily? Come on out here, you two."

This is it.

My final finals. My last comic competition. The last time I'll learn if I'm a winner or a loser.

I know I should be nervous, but I'm not.

Vasily and I join Peter Kay at center stage. Dramatic music thrums out of speakers. A dozen follow spots swish and swoop up and down until they find us and we look like two prisoners caught trying to break out of the state pen.

Peter Kay is holding an awesome, globe-shaped glass trophy.

And Vasily is drooling.

He wants this thing so badly, he sort of reminds me of a younger me. You know, the Jamie Grimm from last night.

Chapter 69

THE PLANET'S FUNNIEST KID COMIC

"**T**he votes have been tabulated," Peter Kay announces as the drums roll. "The winner of the Planet's Funniest Kid Comic worldwide competition is…"

More dramatic music. Tension builds.

Peter Kay opens a thick envelope. Reads it. To himself. He lets a little more tension build. He must really like dramatic drumrolls.

Then, finally, after what seems like a week, he reads it out loud:

"JAMIE GRIMM!"

The audience goes crazy. Confetti, the sparkly kind, shoots out of cannons. Balloons drop.

I reach out to shake Vasily's hand, but he's already gone, stomping offstage.

Peter Kay hands me the laughing globe trophy. "Congratulations, Jamie," he says. "You earned this by being the funniest kid here, not by a sympathy vote."

"Thanks," I say. "But I can't really accept this."

Peter Kay (probably for the first time in his life) is speechless.

So I keep speaking. "Comedy isn't about winners and losers. It's about laughter. The shortest distance between two people. And nobody made me laugh harder than Hamish Gadsby! Hamish, where are you?"

"I don't know!" he shouts from backstage. "I'm blind, remember?"

I'm cracking up. "Get out here, mate. This is yours."

Hamish comes onstage. I give him the trophy. He carefully feels it all over. "Great. A glass basketball with a nose. One shot and SMASH. It's useless. But I want to give this to somebody who made me laugh my glasses off. Chiku Jemaiyo? Where are you? This is now yours."

The Kenyan comic comes onstage and immediately awards the trophy to Benji Yatzpan, who gives it to Fadi Hanania, who gives it to Siobhan Kelly, who hands it off to Demarco Coetzee, who thinks Alfie Hobbes should've won. But Alfie has a soft spot for mimes, so he gives it to Jean-Claude, who gives it to Ichika (he mimes a kitty cat to call her onstage), who gives it to Miguel, who calls Grace Garner up from the audience. And on and on it goes until every single comic from the competition is onstage—well, everybody except Vasily Vasilovich.

At the end of our worldwide tour, we kids have figured out what the best comedians in the world have always known. Laughter should bring people together, not tear them apart. A sense of humor is what humans invented so they could stop hitting each other with sticks and clubs.

Laughter is also what brought me and Gilda together.

I'm pretty sure that if I'd never met her, there would be a lot less laughter in my life.

Boy, I can't wait to head home.

AND IN CONCLUSION...

After my whirlwind tour around the world, I fly home to America wishing my wheelchair were equipped with an odometer. (One of those wrist gadgets that count steps wouldn't really work. Unless it also counts rolls.)

I just wish I had some way to track how far I've come.

Think about it: I went from being the Crip from Cornball to the star of my own TV show. From a hick in the sticks to a hit in Hollywood.

I started my journey scared and alone. Now I'm happy and surrounded by friends and fans and family. In fact, I have a brand-new family—Uncle

Frankie and Aunt Flora. We agreed I can still call him Uncle Frankie even though, officially, he's my new dad. I *am* going to call Aunt Flora Mom, though. She smiles every time I do.

I live in their garage with Uncle Frankie's sweet cherry-red Mustang parked next to my computer table. He says it's going to be mine one day after he adapts it with hand controls. Even though I don't live with the Smileys anymore, they come over for dinner often, and Stevie and I watch comedy shows on TV together. It's incredible how different things are between us.

Plus, I have good friends at home and all over the world now. I keep in touch with all of the world's funniest kid comics over video calls. Sometimes our group calls are so funny we can't hear one another over our laughter. And the one who cracks me up the most?

Vasily Vasilovich.

That's right. After the contest was over and he had no reason to be competitive, he apologized and asked to be friends. He said he'd never had more fun in his entire life than with us.

All of us were more than happy to say yes. People can change, after all.

I know I sure have.

Sometimes I think back to my first kid comic contest in Ronkonkoma. All I could remember were the punch lines to my jokes, but none of the setups.

Now I remember so much.

The sad and frightened kids at the Hope Trust Children's Rehabilitation Center I was able to make smile.

The performance in the hurricane shelter.

The show we did to save the library.

Inviting kids with disabilities to be in the audience of my TV show.

All the fantastic comedians and jokes and laughter.

And, of course, I remember the day I first met Gilda Gold.

How could I forget that? It might turn out to be the most important day in my whole life.

On my first Saturday home, Gilda and I decide to go to the movies. Together. Yes, it's a date. There, I said it!

I hope it's the first of many.

With Gilda in my corner, I know I'll always keep moving forward. Because she'll always be there to push me.

Not my wheelchair. *Me!*

And after the movie, if it looks like Gilda wants to kiss me, guess what?

This time, I'll kiss her first.

About the Authors

James Patterson is the internationally bestselling author of the highly praised Middle School books, *Homeroom Diaries, Kenny Wright: Superhero, Word of Mouse, Pottymouth and Stoopid, Laugh Out Loud, Not So Normal Norbert, Unbelievably Boring Bart, Max Einstein: The Genius Experiment* and the I Funny, Jacky Ha-Ha, Treasure Hunters, Dog Diaries and Max Einstein series. James Patterson's books have sold more than 375 million copies worldwide, making him one of the biggest-selling authors of all time. He lives in Florida.

Chris Grabenstein is a *New York Times* bestselling author who has collaborated with James Patterson on the I Funny, Treasure Hunters, Jacky Ha-Ha and House of Robots series, as well as on *Word of Mouse, Pottymouth and Stoopid, Laugh Out Loud* and *Daniel X: Armageddon.* He lives in New York City.

Jomike Tejido is an author-illustrator who has illustrated more than one hundred children's books. He is based in Manila, and once got into trouble in school for passing around funny cartoons during class. He now does this for a living and shares his jokes with his seven-year-old daughter, Sophia.

TWELVE-YEAR-OLD ORPHAN MAX EINSTEIN IS NOT YOUR TYPICAL GENIUS.

READ ON FOR AN EXTRACT

1

The stench of horse manure woke Max Einstein with a jolt.

"Of course!"

Even though she was shivering, she threw off her blanket and hopped out of bed. Actually, it wasn't really a bed. More like a lumpy, water-stained mattress with frayed seams. But that didn't matter. Ideas could come wherever they wanted.

She raced down the dark hall. The floorboards—bare planks laid across rough beams—creaked and wobbled with every step. Her red hair, of course, was a bouncing tangle of wild curls. It was always a bouncing tangle of wild curls.

Max rapped her knuckles on a lopsided door hanging off rusty hinges.

"Mr. Kennedy?" She knocked again. "Mr. Kennedy?"

"What the…" came a sleepy mumble. "Max? Are you okay?"

Max took that question as permission to enter Mr. Kennedy's apartment. She practically burst through his wonky door.

"I'm fine, Mr. Kennedy. In fact, I'm better than fine! I've got something great here! At least I think it's something great. Anyway, it's really, really cool. This idea could change everything. It could save our world. It's what Mr. Albert Einstein would've called an 'aha' moment."

"Maxine?"

"Yes, Mr. Kennedy?"

"It's six o'clock in the morning, girl."

"Is it? Sorry about the inconvenient hour. But you never know when a brainstorm will strike, do you?"

"No. Not with *you*, anyway…"

Max was wearing a floppy trench coat over her shabby sweater. Lately, she'd been sleeping in the sweater under a scratchy horse blanket because her so-called bedroom was, just like Mr. Kennedy's, extremely cold.

The tall and sturdy black man, his hair flecked with patches of white, creaked out of bed and rubbed some of the sleep out of his eyes. He slid his bare feet into shoes he had fashioned out of cardboard and old newspapers.

"Hang on," he said. "Need to put on my bedroom slippers here…"

"Because the floor's so cold," said Max.

"Huh?"

"You needed to improvise those bedroom slippers because the floor's cold every morning. Correct?"

"Maxine—we're sleeping, uninvited, above a horse stable. Of course the floors are cold. And, in case you haven't noticed, the place doesn't smell so good, either."

Max, Mr. Kennedy, and about a half-dozen other homeless people were what New York City called "squatters." That meant they were living rent-free in the vacant floors above a horse stable. The first two floors of the building housed a parking garage for Central Park carriages and stalls for the horses that pulled them. The top three floors? As far as the owner of the building knew, they were vacant.

"Winter is coming, Mr. Kennedy. We have no central heating system."

"Nope. We sure don't. You know why? Because we don't pay rent, Max!"

"Be that as it may, in the coming weeks, these floors will only become colder. Soon, we could all freeze to death. Even if we were to board up all the windows—"

"That's not gonna happen," said Mr. Kennedy. "We

need the ventilation. All that horse manure downstairs, stinking up the place…"

"Exactly! That's precisely what I wanted to talk to you about. That's my big idea. *Horse manure!*"

2

"It's simple, really, Mr. Kennedy," said Max, moving to the cracked plaster wall and finding a patch that wasn't covered with graffiti.

She pulled a thick stub of chalk out her baggy sweater pocket and started sketching on the wall, turning it into her blackboard.

"Please hear me out, sir. Try to see what I see."

Max, who enjoyed drawing in a beat-up sketchbook she rescued from a Dumpster, chalked in a lump of circles radiating stink marks. She labeled it "manure/biofuel."

"To stay warm this winter, all we have to do is arrange a meeting with Mr. Sammy Monk."

"The owner of this building?" said Mr. Kennedy,

skeptically. "The landlord who doesn't even know we're here? *That* Mr. Sammy Monk?"

"Yes, sir," said Max, totally engrossed in the diagram she was drafting on the wall. "We need to convince him to let us have all of his horse manure."

Mr. Kennedy stood up. "All of his manure? Now why on earth would we want that, Max? It's manure!"

"Well, once we have access to the manure, I will design and engineer a green gas mill for the upstairs apartments."

"A green what mill?"

"Gas, sir. We can rig up an anaerobic digester that will turn the horse manure into biogas, which we can then combust to generate electricity and heat."

"You want to burn horse manure gas?"

"Exactly! Anaerobic digestion is a series of biological processes in which microorganisms break down biodegradable material, such as horse manure, in the absence of oxygen, which is what 'anaerobic' means. That's the solution to our heating and power problems."

"You sure you're just twelve years old?"

"Yes. As far as I know."

Mr. Kennedy gave Max a look that she, unfortunately, was used to seeing. The look said she was crazy. Nuts. Off her rocker. But Max never let "the look" upset her. It was like Albert Einstein said, "Great spirits have always encountered violent opposition from mediocre minds."

Not that Mr. Kennedy had a mediocre mind. Max just wasn't doing a good enough job explaining her bold new breakthrough idea. Sometimes, the ideas came into her head so fast they came out of her mouth in a mumbled jumble.

"All we need, Mr. Kennedy, is an airtight container—something between the size of an oil drum and a tanker truck." She sketched a boxy cube fenced in by a pen of steel posts. "Heavy plastic would be best, of course. And it would be good if it had a cage of galvanized iron bars surrounding it. Then we just have to measure and cut three different pipes—one for feeding in the manure, one for the gas outlet, and one for displaced liquid fertilizer. We would insert these conduits into the tank through a universal seal, hook up the appropriate plumbing, and we'd be good to go."

Mr. Kennedy stroked his stubbly chin and admired Max's detailed design of the device sketched on the flaking wall.

"A brilliant idea, Max," he said. "Like always."

Max allowed herself a small, proud smile.

"Thank you, Mr. Kennedy."

"Slight problem."

"What's that, sir?"

"Well, that container there. The cube. That's what? Ten feet by ten feet by ten feet?"

"About."

"And you say you need a cage of bars around it. You also mentioned three pipes. And plumbing. Then I figure you're going to need a furnace to burn the horse manure gas, turn it into heat."

Max nodded. "And a generator. To spin our own electricity."

"Right. Won't that cost a whole lot of money?"

Max lowered her chalk. "I suppose so."

"And have you ever noticed the one thing most people squatting in this building don't have?"

Max pursed her lips. "Money?"

"Uhm-hmm. Exactly."

Max tucked the stubby chalk back into her sweater pocket and dusted off her pale, cold hands.

"Point taken, Mr. Kennedy. As usual, I need to be more practical. I'll get back to you with a better plan. I'll get back to you before winter comes."

"Great. But, Max?"

"Yes, sir?"

Mr. Kennedy climbed back into his lumpy bed and pulled up the blanket.

"Just don't get back to me before seven o'clock, okay?"

3

Max glanced at her watch.

It was only 6:17 a.m. She, unlike Mr. Kennedy, was an early riser. Always had been, probably always would be. The morning, especially that quiet space between dreaming and total wakefulness, was when most of her massive ideas floated through her drowsy brain. The ideas helped tamp down the sadness that could come in those same quiet times. A sadness that all orphans probably shared. Made more intense because Max had no idea who either of her parents were.

Max creaked her way back up the hall to her room as quietly as she could. She could hear Mr. Kennedy already snoring behind her.

Max had decorated her own sleeping space in the stables

building the same way she had decorated all the rooms she had ever temporarily lived in: by propping open her battered old suitcase on its side to turn it into a display case for all things Albert Einstein. Books by and about the famous scientist were lined along the bottom like a bookshelf. Both lids were filled with her collection of Einstein photographs and quotes. She even had an Einstein bobblehead doll she'd found, once upon a time, in a museum store dumpster. She used it as a bookend.

Max couldn't remember where the suitcase came from. She'd just always had it. It was older than her rumpled knit sweater, and that thing was an antique.

The oldest photograph in her collection, the one that someone other than Max (she didn't know who) had pasted inside the suitcase lid so long ago that its edges were curling, showed the great professor lost in thought. He had a bushy mustache and long, unkempt hair. His hands were clasped together, almost as if in prayer. His eyes were gazing up toward infinity.

That photograph was Max's oldest memory. And since she never knew her own parents, at an early age, Max found herself talking to the kind, grandfatherly man at bedtime. He was a very good listener. She became curious as to who the mystery man might be, and that's how her lifelong infatuation with all things Einstein began.

Like how he was born in Germany but had to leave his home before the Second World War. And how he was so busy thinking of big, amazing ideas, he sometimes forgot to pay attention to his job at the patent office. They had a lot in common.

Next to the photograph was Max's absolute favorite Einstein quote: "Imagination is more important than knowledge."

"Unless, of course, you don't have the money to make the things you dream up come true," Max muttered.

Mr. Kennedy was right.

She couldn't afford to build her green gas mill. And she couldn't ask Mr. Sammy Monk for his horse manure or anything else because Mr. Sammy Monk couldn't know anybody was living in the abandoned floors of his horse stable. She'd just have to imagine a different solution to the squatters' heating dilemma. One that didn't cost a dime and could be created out of someone else's discarded scraps.

Max turned to her computer, which she had built herself from found parts. It was amazing what some people in New York City tossed to the curb on garbage pickup days. Max had been able to solder together (with a perfectly good soldering iron someone had thrown out) enough discarded circuit boards, unwanted wiring, abandoned processors, rejected keyboards, and one slightly blemished retina screen from a cast-off MacBook Pro to create a machine that whirred even faster than her mind.

She also had free wi-fi, thanks to the Link NYC public hot spot system. She could even recharge her computer's batteries (discovered abandoned behind one of the city's glossy Apple stores) at the kiosk just down the block from the stables. (Reliable wi-fi was one of the main reasons Max had selected her current accommodations. Easy access to a top-flight school was the other.)

Max clicked open a browser and went back to the internet page she had bookmarked the night before.

It was a nightmarish news report about children as young as seven "working in perilous conditions in the Democratic Republic of the Congo to mine cobalt that ends up in smartphones, cars, and computers sold to millions across the world." The children, as many as forty thousand, were being paid one dollar a day to do backbreaking work. They were also helping make a shadowy international business consortium called the Corp very, very, *very* rich.

The story broke Max's heart.

Because Max's heart, like her hero Dr. Einstein's, was huge.

The
I FUNNY
SERIES

I FUNNY
(with Chris Grabenstein)
Join Jamie Grimm at middle school where he's on
an unforgettable mission to win the Planet's Funniest
Kid Comic Contest. Dealing with the school bully
(who he also happens to live with) and coping with
a disability are no trouble for Jamie when
he has laughter on his side.

I EVEN FUNNIER
(with Chris Grabenstein)
Heading to the national semi-finals, Jamie's one
step closer to achieving his dream! But will a sudden
family health scare put his ambitions on hold?

I TOTALLY FUNNIEST
(with Chris Grabenstein)
Jamie's heading to Hollywood for his biggest
challenge yet. There's only the small matter of the
national finals and eight other laugh-a-minute
competitors between him and the
trophy—oh, and a hurricane!

I FUNNY TV
(with Chris Grabenstein)
Jamie has achieved his dream of becoming the
Planet's Funniest Kid Comic, and now the sky's the
limit! Enter a couple of TV executives with an offer
for Jamie to star in his very own show...

SCHOOL OF LAUGHS
(with Chris Grabenstein)
Jamie has a national contest trophy and a TV
show under his belt, but teaching other kids how to be
funny is the toughest gig that he has ever had. And
if he fails, his school library will be shut
down for good!

ALSO BY JAMES PATTERSON

MIDDLE SCHOOL BOOKS
The Worst Years of My Life (*with Chris Tebbetts*)
Get Me Out of Here! (*with Chris Tebbetts*)
My Brother Is a Big, Fat Liar (*with Lisa Papademetriou*)
How I Survived Bullies, Broccoli, and Snake Hill
(*with Chris Tebbetts*)
Ultimate Showdown (*with Julia Bergen*)
Save Rafe! (*with Chris Tebbetts*)
Just My Rotten Luck (*with Chris Tebbetts*)
Dog's Best Friend (*with Chris Tebbetts*)
Escape to Australia (*with Martin Chatterton*)
From Hero to Zero (*with Chris Tebbetts*)

DOG DIARIES SERIES

Dog Diaries (*with Steven Butler*)
Happy Howlidays (*with Steven Butler*)

TREASURE HUNTERS SERIES

Treasure Hunters (*with Chris Grabenstein*)
Danger Down the Nile (*with Chris Grabenstein*)
Secret of the Forbidden City (*with Chris Grabenstein*)
Peril at the Top of the World (*with Chris Grabenstein*)
Quest for the City of Gold (*with Chris Grabenstein*)

HOUSE OF ROBOTS SERIES

House of Robots (*with Chris Grabenstein*)
Robots Go Wild! (*with Chris Grabenstein*)
Robot Revolution (*with Chris Grabenstein*)

JACKY HA-HA SERIES

Jacky Ha-Ha (*with Chris Grabenstein*)
My Life is a Joke (*with Chris Grabenstein*)

OTHER ILLUSTRATED NOVELS

Kenny Wright: Superhero (*with Chris Tebbetts*)
Homeroom Diaries (*with Lisa Papademetriou*)
Word of Mouse (*with Chris Grabenstein*)
Pottymouth and Stoopid (*with Chris Grabenstein*)
Laugh Out Loud (*with Chris Grabenstein*)
Not So Normal Norbert (*with Joey Green*)
Unbelievably Boring Bart (*with Duane Swierczynski*)
Max Einstein: The Genius Experiment
(*with Chris Grabenstein*)

For more information about James Patterson's novels,
visit www.jamespatterson.co.uk